HAMLET, PRINCE OF DENMARK

William Shakespeare, the great English playwright, was born in 1564. He was a leading member of Lord Chamberlain's Men, which later became the King's Men, a company of actors. He died in 1616 and was buried in Holy Trinity Church, Stratford-upon-Avon.

HAMLET, PRINCE OF DENMARK

William Shakespeare

RUPA

Published by
Rupa Publications India Pvt. Ltd 2004
7/16, Ansari Road, Daryaganj
New Delhi 110002

Sales centres:
Allahabad Bengaluru Chennai
Hyderabad Jaipur Kathmandu
Kolkata Mumbai

This is a work of fiction. Names, characters, places and incidents
are either the product of the author's imagination or are used
fictitiously and any resemblance to any actual person, living or dead,
events or locales is entirely coincidental.

ISBN: 978-81-291-0605-6

Eighth impression 2019

10 9 8

DRAMATIS PERSONAE

CLAUDIUS, *King of Denmark.*
HAMLET, *son to the former and nephew to the present King.*

POLONIUS,	*Lord Chamberlain.*
HORATIO,	*friend to Hamlet.*
LAERTES,	*son to Polonius.*

VOLTEMAND,
CORNELIUS,
ROSENCRANTZ,   *courtiers.*
GUILDENSTERN,
OSRIC,
A GENTLEMAN,
A PRIEST.

MARCELLUS,
BERNARDO,   *officers.*

FRANCISCO,   *a soldier.*
REYNALDO,   *servant to Polonius.*
Players.
Two Clowns,   *grave-diggers.*
FORTINBRAS,   *Prince of Norway.*
A Norwegian Captain.
English Ambassadors.
GERTRUDE, *Queen of Denmark, and mother of Hamlet.*
OPHELIA, *daughter to Polonius.*
Ghost of Hamlet's Father.
Lords, Ladies, Officers, Soldiers, Sailors, Messengers, *and* Attendants.

THE SCENE : *Denmark.*

ACT I SCENE I

Elsinore. The guard-platform of the Castle.

FRANCISCO AT HIS POST. ENTER TO HIM BERNARDO.

BER.	Who's there?
FRAN.	Nay, answer me. Stand and unfold yourself.
BER.	Long live the King !
FRAN.	Bernardo?
BER.	He.
FRAN.	You come most carefully upon your hour.
BER.	'Tis now struck twelve; get thee to bed, Francisco.
FRAN.	For this relief much thanks. 'Tis bitter cold, And I am sick at heart.
BER.	Have you had quiet guard?

FRAN.	Not a mouse stirring.
BER.	Well, good night.
	If you do meet Horatio and Marcellus,
	The rivals of my watch, bid them make haste.

ENTER HORATIO AND MARCELLUS.

FRAN.	I think I hear them. Stand, ho! Who is there?
HOR.	Friends to this ground.
MAR.	And liegemen to the Dane.
FRAN.	Give you good night.
MAR.	O, farewell, honest soldier! Who hath reliev'd you?
FRAN.	Bernardo hath my place. Give you good night.
	[*Exit.*
MAR.	Holla, Bernado!
BER.	Say—
	What, is Horatio there?
HOR.	A piece of him.
BER.	Welcome, Horatio; welcome, good Marcellus.
HOR.	What, has this thing appear'd again to-night?
BER.	I have seen nothing.
MAR.	Horatio says 'tis but our fantasy,
	And will not let belief take hold of him
	Touching this dreaded sight, twice seen of us;
	Therefore I have entreated him along
	With us to watch the minutes of this night,
	That, if again this apparition come,

He may approve our eyes and speak to it.

HOR. Tush, tush, 'twill not appear.

BER. Sit down awhile,
And let us once again assail your ears,
That are so fortified against our story,
What we have two nights seen.

HOR. Well, sit we down,
And let us hear Bernardo speak of this.

BER. Last night of all,
When yond same star that's westward from
the pole
Had made his course t' illume that part of
heaven
Where now it burns, Marcellus and myself,
The bell then beating one—

ENTER GHOST.

MAR. Peace, break thee off; look where it comes
again.

BER. In the same figure, like the King that's dead.

MAR. Thou art a scholar; speak to it, Horatio.

BER. Looks 'a not like the King? Mark it, Horatio.

HOR. Most like. It harrows me with fear and
wonder.

BER. It would be spoke to.

MAR. Question it, Horatio.

HOR. What art thou that usurp'st this time of night
Together with that fair and warlike form

In which the majesty of buried Denmark
Did sometimes march? By heaven I charge
thee, speak!

MAR.   It is offended.

BER.   See, it stalks away.

HOR.   Stay! speak, speak! I charge thee, speak!

[*Exit Ghost.*

MAR.   'Tis gone, and will not answer.

BER.   How now, Horatio! You tremble and look
pale.
Is not this something more than fantasy?
What think you on't?

HOR.   Before my God, I might not this believe
Without the sensible and true avouch
Of mine own eyes.

MAR.   Is it not like the King?

HOR.   As thou art to thyself:
Such was the very armour he had on
When he the ambitious Norway combated;
So frown'd he once when, in an angry parle,
He smote the sledded Polacks on the ice.
'Tis strange.

MAR.   Thus twice before, and jump at this dead
hour,
With martial stalk hath he gone by our watch.

HOR.   In what particular thought to work I know
not;
But, in the gross and scope of mine opinion,
This bodes some strange eruption to our state.

MAR. Good now, sit down, and tell me, he that
knows,
Why this same strict and most observant
watch
So nightly toils the subject of.the land;
And why such daily cast of brazen cannon,
And foreign mart for implements of war;
Why such impress of shipwrights, whose sore
task
Does not divide the Sunday from the week;
What might be toward, that this sweaty haste
Doth make the night join-labourer with the
day:
Who is't that can inform me?

HOR. That can I;
At least, the whisper goes so. Our last king,
Whose image even but now appear'd to us,
Was, as you know, by Fortinbras of Norway,
Thereto prick'd on by a most emulate pride,
Dar'd to the combat; in which our valiant
Hamlet—
For so this side of our known world esteem'd
him—
Did slay this Fortinbras; who, by a seal'd
compact,
Well ratified by law and heraldry,
Did forfeit, with his life, all those his lands
Which he stood seiz'd of, to the conqueror;
Against the which a moiety competent

Was gaged by our king; which had return'd
To the inheritance of Fortinbras,
Had he been vanquisher; as, by the same comart
And carriage of the article design'd,
His fell to Hamlet. Now, sir, young Fortinbras,
Of unimproved mettle hot and full,
Hath in the skirts of Norway, here and there,
Shark'd up a list of lawless resolutes,
For food and diet, to some enterprise
That hath a stomach in't; which is no other,
As it doth well appear unto our state,
But to recover us, by strong hand
And terms compulsatory, those foresaid lands
So by his father lost; and this, I take it,
Is the main motive of our preparations,
The source of this our watch, and the chief head
Of this post-haste and romage in the land.

BER. I think it be no other but e'en so.
Well may it sort, that this portentous figure
Comes armed through our watch; so like the King
That was and is the question of these wars.

HOR. A mote it is to trouble the mind's eye.
In the most high and palmy state of Rome,
A little ere the mightiest Julius fell,
The graves stood tenantless, and the sheeted

dead
Did squeak and gibber in the Roman streets;
As, stars with trains of fire, and dews of blood,
Disasters in the sun; and the moist star
Upon whose influence Neptune's empire
stands
Was sick almost to doomsday with eclipse;
And even the like precurse of fear'd events,
As harbingers preceding still the fates
And prologue to the omen coming on,
Have heaven and earth together demon-
strated
Unto our climatures and countrymen.

RE-ENTER GHOST.

But, soft, behold! Lo, where it comes again!
I'll cross it, though it blast me. Stay, illusion.
                    [*Ghost spreads its arms.*
If thou hast any sound or use of voice,
Speak to me.
If there be any good thing to be done,
That may to thee do ease and grace to me,
Speak to me.
If thou art privy to thy country's fate,
Which happily foreknowing may avoid,
O, speak!
Or if thou hast uphoarded in thy life
Extorted treasure in the womb of earth,
For which, they say, you spirits oft walk in

death,   [*The cock crows.*
Speak of it. Stay, and speak. Stop it,
Marcellus.

MAR.   Shall I strike at it with my partisan?

HOR.   Do, if it will not stand.

BER.   'Tis here!

HOR.   'Tis here!

MAR.   'Tis gone!   [*Exit Ghost.*
We do it wrong, being so majestical,
To offer it the show of violence;
For it is, as the air, invulnerable,
And our vain blows malicious mockery.

BER.   It was about to speak, when the cock crew.

HOR.   And then it started like a guilty thing
Upon a fearful summons. I have heard
The cock, that is the trumpet to the morn,
Doth with his lofty and shrill-sounding throat
Awake the god of day; and at his warning,
Whether in sea or fire, in earth or air,
Th' extravagant and erring spirit hies
To his confine; and of the truth herein
This present object made probation.

MAR.   It faded on the crowing of the cock.
Some say that ever 'gainst that season comes
Wherein our Saviour's birth is celebrated,
This bird of dawning singeth all night long;
And then, they say, no spirit dare stir abroad,
The nights are wholesome, then no planets
strike,

No fairy takes, nor witch hath power to charm,
So hallowed and so gracious is that time.

HOR. So have I heard, and do in part believe it.
Bat look, the morn, in russet mantle clad,
Walks o'er the dew of yon high eastward hill.
Break we our watch up; and, by my advice,
Let us impart what we have seen to-night
Unto young Hamlet; for, upon my life,
This spirit, dumb to us, will speak to him.
Do you consent we shall acquaint him with it,
As needful in our loves, fitting our duty?

MAR. Let's do't, I pray; and I this morning know
Where we shall find him most convenient.
[*Exeunt.*

SCENE II

Elsinore. The Castle.

FLOURISH. ENTER CLAUDIUS KING OF DENMARK,
GERTRUDE THE QUEEN, AND COUNCILLORS,
INCLUDING POLONIUS, HIS SON LAERTES, VOLTEMAND,
CORNELIUS, AND HAMLET.

KING. Though yet of Hamlet our dear brother's death

The memory be green; and that it us befitted
To bear our hearts in grief, and our whole kingdom
To be contracted in one brow of woe;
Yet so far hath discretion fought with nature
That we with wisest sorrow think on him,
Together with remembrance of ourselves.
Therefore our sometime sister, now our queen,
Th' imperial jointress to this warlike state,
Have we, as 'twere with a defeated joy,
With an auspicious and a dropping eye,
With mirth in funeral, and with dirge in marriage,
In equal scale weighing delight and dole,
Taken to wife; nor have we herein barr'd
Your better wisdoms, which have freely gone
With this affair along. For all, our thanks.
Now follows that you know: young Fortinbras,
Holding a weak supposal of our worth,
Or thinking by our late dear brother's death
Our state to be disjoint and out of frame,
Co-leagued with this dream of his advantage—
He hath not fail'd to pester us with message
Importing the surrender of those lands
Lost by his father, with all bands of law,

To our most valiant brother. So much for him.
Now for ourself, and for this time of meeting,
Thus much the business is: we have here writ
To Norway, uncle of young Fortinbras—
Who, impotent and bed-rid, scarcely hears
Of this his nephew's purpose—to suppress
His further gait herein, in that the levies,
The lists, and full proportions, are all made
Out of his subject; and we here dispatch
You, good Cornelius, and you, Voltemand,
For bearers of this greeting to old Norway;
Giving to you no further personal power
To business with the King more than the scope
Of these delated articles allow.
Farewell; and let your haste commend your duty.

COR. ⎫
VOL. ⎬ In that and all things will we show our duty.
         ⎭

KING.   We doubt it nothing, heartily farewell.
              [*Exeunt Voltemand and Cornelius.*
        And now, Laertes, what's the news with you?
        You told us of some suit; what is't, Laertes?
        You cannot speak of reason to the Dane
        And lose your voice. What wouldst thou beg, Laertes,
        That shall not be my offer, not thy asking?

The head is not more native to the heart,
The hand more instrumental to the mouth,
Than is the throne of Denmark to thy father.
What wouldst thou have, Laertes?

LAER.   My dread lord,
Your leave and favour to return to France;
From whence though willingly I came to Denmark
To show my duty in your coronation,
Yet now, I must confess, that duty done,
My thoughts and wishes bend again toward France,
And bow them to your gracious leave and pardon.

KING.   Have you your father's leave? What says Polonius?

POL.   'A hath, my lord, wrung from me my slow leave
By laboursome petition; and at last
Upon his will I seal'd my hard consent.
I do beseech you, give him leave to go.

KING.   Take thy fair hour, Laertes; time be thine,
And thy best graces spend it at thy will!
But now, my cousin Hamlet, and my son—

HAM.   [Aside] A little more than kin, and less than kind.

KING.   How is it that the clouds still hang on you?

HAM.   Not so, my lord; I am too much in the sun.

QUEEN.   Good Hamlet, cast thy nighted colour off,
         And let thine eye look like a friend on
         Denmark.
         Do not for ever with thy vailed lids
         Seek for thy noble father in the dust.
         Thou know'st 'tis common—all that lives
         must die,
         Passing through nature to eternity.

HAM.   Ay, madam, it is common.

QUEEN.   If it be,
         Why seems it so particular with thee?

HAM.   Seems, madam! Nay, it is; I know not seems.
         'Tis not alone my inky cloak, good mother,
         Nor customary suits of solemn black,
         Nor windy suspiration of forc'd breath,
         No, nor the fruitful river in the eye,
         Nor the dejected haviour of the visage,
         Together with all forms, moods, shapes of
         grief,
         That can denote me truly. These, indeed,
         seem;
         For they are actions that a man might play;
         But I have that within which passes show—
         These but the trappings and the suits of woe.

KING.   'Tis sweet and commendable in your nature,
         Hamlet,
         To give these mourning duties to your father;
         But you must know your father lost a father;

That father lost his; and the survivor bound,
In filial obligation, for some term
To do obsequious sorrow. But to persever
In obstinate condolement is a course
Of impious stubbornness; 'tis unmanly grief;
It shows a will most incorrect to heaven,
A heart unfortified, a mind impatient,
An understanding simple and unschool'd;
For what we know must be, and is as
common
As any the most vulgar thing to sense,
Why should we in our peevish opposition
Take it to heart? Fie! 'tis a fault to heaven,
A fault against the dead, a fault to nature,
To reason most absurd; whose common
theme
Is death of fathers, and who still hath cried,
From the first corse till he that died to-day,
'This must be so'. We pray you throw to earth
This unprevailing woe, and think of us
As of a father; for let the world take note
You are the most immediate to our throne;
And with no less nobility of love
Than that which dearest father bears his son
Do I impart toward you. For your intent
In going back to school in Wittenberg,
It is most retrograde to our desire;
And we beseech you bend you to remain
Here, in the cheer and comfort of our eye,

	Our chiefest courtier, cousin, and our son.

QUEEN. Let not thy mother lose her prayers, Hamlet:
I pray thee stay with us; go not to Wittenberg.

HAM. I shall in all my best obey you, madam.

KING. Why, 'tis a loving and a fair reply.
Be as ourself in Denmark. Madam, come;
This gentle and unforc'd accord of Hamlet
Sits smiling to my heart; in grace whereof,
No jocund health that Denmark drinks to-day
But the great cannon to the clouds shall tell,
And the King's rouse the heaven shall bruit again,
Re-speaking earthly thunder. Come away.
      [*Flourish. Exeunt all but Hamlet.*

HAM. O, that this too too solid flesh would melt,
Thaw, and resolve itself into a dew!
Or that the Everlasting had not fix'd
His canon 'gainst self-slaughter! O God! God!
How weary, stale, flat, and unprofitable,
Seem to me all the uses of this world!
Fie on't! Ah, fie! 'tis an unweeded garden,
That grows to seed; things rank and gross in nature
Possess it merely. That it should come to this!
But two months dead! Nay, not so much, not two.
So excellent a king that was to this
Hyperion to a satyr; so loving to my mother,

That he might not beteem the winds of
heaven
Visit her face too roughly. Heaven and earth!
Must I remember? Why, she would hang on
him
As if increase of appetite had grown
By what it fed on; and yet, within a month—
Let me not think on't. Frailty, thy name is
woman!—
A little month, or ere those shoes were old
With which she followed my poor father's
body,
Like Niobe, all tears—why she, even she—
O God! a beast that wants discourse of reason
Would have mourn'd longer—married with
my uncle,
My father's brother; but no more like my
father
Than I to Hercules. Within a month,
Ere yet the salt of most unrighteous tears
Had left the flushing in her galled eyes,
She married. O, most wicked speed, to post
With such dexterity to incestuous sheets!
It is not, nor it cannot come to good.
But break, my heart, for I must hold my
tongue.

ENTER HORATIO, MARCELLUS, AND BERNARDO.

HOR.   Hail to your lordship!

HAM.   I am glad to see you well.
       Horatio—or I do forget myself.
HOR.   The same, my lord, and your poor servant
       ever.
HAM.   Sir, my good friend. I'll change that name
       with you.
       And what make you from Wittenberg,
       Horatio?
       Marcellus?
MAR.   My good lord!
HAM.   I am very glad to see you. [*To Bernardo*] Good
       even, sir.—
       But what, in faith, make you from Witten-
       berg?
HOR.   A truant disposition, good my lord.
HAM.   I would not hear your enemy say so;
       Nor shall you do my ear that violence,
       To make it truster of your own report
       Against yourself. I know you are not truant.
       But what is your affair in Elsinore?
       We'll teach you to drink deep ere you depart.
HOR.   My lord, I came to see your father's funeral.
HAM.   I prithee do not mock me, fellow-student;
       I think it was to see my mother's wedding.
HOR.   Indeed, my lord, it followed hard upon.
HAM.   Thrift, thrift, Horatio! The funeral bak'd-
       meats
       Did coldly furnish forth the marriage tables.

Would I had met my dearest foe in heaven
Or ever I had seen that day, Horatio!
My father—methinks I see my father.

HOR.   Where, my lord?

HAM.   In my mind's eye, Horatio.

HOR.   I saw him once; 'a was a goodly king.

HAM.   'A was a man, take him for all in all,
I shall not look upon his like again.

HOR.   My lord, I think I saw him yesternight.

HAM.   Saw who?

HOR.   My lord, the King your father.

HAM.   The King my father!

HOR.   Season your admiration for a while
With an attent ear, till I may deliver,
Upon the witness of these gentlemen,
This marvel to you.

HAM.   For God's love, let me hear.

HOR.   Two nights together had these gentlemen,
Marcellus and Bernardo, on their watch,
In the dead waste and middle of the night,
Been thus encount'red. A figure like your father,
Armed at point exactly, cap-a-pe,
Appears before them, and with solemn march
Goes slow and stately by them; thrice he walk'd
By their oppress'd and fear-surprised eyes,
Within his truncheon's length; whilst they, distill'd

Almost to jelly with the act of fear,
Stand dumb and speak not to him. This to me
In dreadful secrecy impart they did;
And I with them the third night kept the watch;
Where, as they had delivered, both in time,
Form of the thing, each word made true and good,
The apparition comes. I knew your father;
These hands are not more like.

HAM.   But where was this?

MAR.   My lord, upon the platform where we watch.

HAM.   Did you not speak to it?

HOR.   My lord, I did;
But answer made it none; yet once methought
It lifted up it head and did address
Itself to motion, like as it would speak;
But even then the morning cock crew loud,
And at the sound it shrunk in haste away
And vanish'd from our sight.

HAM.   'Tis very strange.

HOR.   As I do live, my honour'd lord, 'tis true;
And we did think it writ down in our duty
To let you know of it.

HAM.   Indeed, indeed, sirs, but this troubles me.
Hold you the watch to-night?

ALL.   We do, my lord.

HAM.	Arm'd, say you?
ALL.	Arm'd, my lord.
HAM.	From top to toe?
ALL.	My lord, from head to foot.
HAM.	Then saw you not his face?
HOR.	O yes, my lord; he wore his beaver up.
HAM.	What, look'd he frowningly?
HOR.	A countenance more in sorrow than in anger.
HAM.	Pale or red?
HOR.	Nay, very pale.
HAM.	And fix'd his eyes upon you?
HOR.	Most constantly.
HAM.	I would I had been there.
HOR.	It would have much amaz'd you.
HAM.	Very like, very like. Stay'd it long?
HOR.	While one with moderate haste might tell a hundred.
BOTH.	Longer, longer.
HOR.	Not when I saw't.
HAM.	His beard was grizzl'd—no?
HOR.	It was, as I have seen it in his life, A sable silver'd.
HAM.	I will watch to-night; Perchance 'twill walk again.
HOR.	I warr'nt it will.
HAM.	If it assume my noble father's person, I'll speak to it, though hell itself should gape And bid me hold my peace. I pray you all,

If you have hitherto conceal'd this sight,
Let it be tenable in your silence still;
And whatsomever else shall hap to-night,
Give it an understanding, but no tongue;
I will requite your loves. So, fare you well—
Upon the platform, 'twixt eleven and twelve,
I'll visit you.

ALL.   Our duty to your honour.

HAM.   Your loves, as mine to you; farewell.

[Exeunt all but Hamlet.

My father's spirit in arms! All is not well.
I doubt some foul play. Would the night were come!
Till then sit still, my soul. Foul deeds will rise,
Though all the earth o'erwhelm them, to men's eyes.   *[Exit.*

SCENE III

Elsinore. The house of Polonius.

ENTER LAERTES AND OPHELIA HIS SISTER.

LAER.   My necessaries are embark'd,
Farewell.
And, sister, as the winds give benefit
And convoy is assistant, do not sleep,

	But let me hear from you.
OPH.	Do you doubt that?
LAER.	For Hamlet, and the trifling of his favour,
	Hold it a fashion and a toy in blood,
	A violet in the youth of primy nature,
	Forward not permanent, sweet not lasting,
	The perfume and suppliance of a minute;
	No more.
OPH.	No more but so?
LAER.	Think it no more;
	For nature crescent does not grow alone
	In thews and bulk, but as this temple waxes,
	The inward service of the mind and soul
	Grows wide withal. Perhaps he loves you now,
	And now no soil nor cautel doth besmirch
	The virtue of his will; but you must fear,
	His greatness weigh'd, his will is not his own;
	For he himself is subject to his birth:
	He may not, as unvalued persons do,
	Carve for himself; for on his choice depends
	The sanity and health of this whole state;
	And therefore must his choice be circum-
	scrib'd
	Unto the voice and yielding of that body
	Whereof he is the head. Then if he says he
	loves you,
	It fits your wisdom so far to believe it
	As he in his particular act and place
	May give his saying deed; which is no further

Than the main voice of Denmark goes withal.
Then weigh what loss your honour may sustain,
If with too credent ear you list his songs,
Or lose your heart, or your chaste treasure open
To his unmast'red importunity.
Fear it, Ophelia, fear it, my dear sister;
And keep you in the rear of your affection,
Out of the shot and danger of desire.
The chariest maid is prodigal enough
If she unmask her beauty to the moon.
Virtue itself scapes not calumnious strokes;
The canker galls the infants of the spring
Too oft before their buttons be disclos'd;
And in the morn and liquid dew of youth
Contagious blastments are most imminent.
Be wary, then; best safety lies in fear:
Youth to itself rebels, though none else near.

OPH.   I shall the effect of this good lesson keep
As watchman to my heart. But, good my brother,
Do not, as some ungracious pastors do,
Show me the steep and thorny way to heaven,
Whiles, like a puff'd and reckless libertine,
Himself the primrose path of dalliance treads
And recks not his own rede.

LAER.   O, fear me not!

ENTER POLONIUS.

I stay too long. But here my father comes.
A double blessing is a double grace;
Occasion smiles upon a second leave.

POL.   Yet here, Laertes! Aboard, aboard, for shame!
The wind sits in the shoulder of your sail,
And you are stay'd for. There—my blessing
with thee!
And these few precepts in thy memory
Look thou character. Give thy thoughts no
tongue,
Nor any unproportion'd thought his act.
Be thou familiar, but by no means vulgar.
Those friends thou hast, and their adoption
tried,
Grapple them to thy soul with hoops of steel;
But do not dull thy palm with entertainment
Of each new-hatch'd, unfledg'd courage.
Beware
Of entrance to a quarrel; but, being in,
Bear't that th' opposed may beware of thee.
Give every man thy ear, but few thy voice;
Take each man's censure, but reserve thy
judgment.
Costly thy habit as thy purse can buy,
But not express'd in fancy; rich, not gaudy;
For the apparel oft proclaims the man;
And they in France of the best rank and station

Are of a most select and generous choice in
that.
Neither a borrower nor a lender be;
For loan oft loses both itself and friend,
And borrowing dulls the edge of husbandry.
This above all—to thine own self be true,
And it must follow, as the night the day,
Thou canst not then be false to any man.
Farewell; my blessing season this in thee!

LAER.	Most humbly do I take my leave, my lord.
POL.	The time invites you; go, your servants tend.
LAER.	Farewell, Ophelia; and remember well What I have said to you.
OPH.	'Tis in my memory lock'd, And you yourself shall keep the key of it.
LAER.	Farewell. [*Exit.*
POL.	What is't, Ophelia, he hath said to you?
OPH.	So please you, something touching the Lord Hamlet.
POL.	Marry, well bethought! 'Tis told me he hath very oft of late Given private time to you; and you yourself Have of your audience been most free and bounteous. If it be so—as so 'tis put on me, And that in way of caution—I must tell you You do not understand yourself so clearly As it behoves my daughter and your honour.

	What is between you? Give me up the truth.
OPH.	He hath, my lord, of late made many tenders
	Of his affection to me.
POL.	Affection! Pooh! You speak like a green girl,
	Unsifted in such perilous circumstance.
	Do you believe his tenders, as you call them?
OPH.	I do not know, my lord, what I should think.
POL.	Marry, I will teach you: think yourself a baby
	That you have ta'en these tenders for true pay
	Which are not sterling. Tender yourself more dearly;
	Or—not to crack the wind of the poor phrase,
	Running it thus—you'll tender me a fool.
OPH.	My lord, he hath importun'd me with love
	In honourable fashion.
POL.	Ay, fashion you may call it; go to, go to.
OPH.	And hath given countenance to his speech, my lord,
	With almost all the holy vows of heaven.
POL.	Ay, springes to catch woodcocks! I do know,
	When the blood burns, how prodigal the soul
	Lends the tongue vows. These blazes, daughter,
	Giving more light than heat—extinct in both,
	Even in their promise, as it is a-making—
	You must not take for fire. From this time
	Be something scanter of your maiden presence;

Set your entreatments at a higher rate
Than a command to parle. For Lord Hamlet,
Believe so much in him, that he is young,
And with a larger tether may he walk
Than may be given you. In few, Ophelia,
Do not believe his vows; for they are brokers,
Not of that dye which their investments
show,
But mere implorators of unholy suits,
Breathing like sanctified and pious bonds,
The better to beguile. This is for all—
I would not, in plain terms, from this time
forth
Have you so slander any moment leisure
As to give words or talk with the Lord
Hamlet.
Look to't, I charge you. Come your ways.

OPH.   I shall obey, my lord.   [*Exeunt.*

SCENE IV

Elsinore. The guard-platform of the Castle.

ENTER HAMLET, HORATIO, AND MARCELLUS.

HAM.   The air bites shrewdly; it is very cold.
HOR.   It is a nipping and an eager air.

HAM.   What hour now?

HOR.   I think it lacks of twelve.

MAR.   No, it is struck.

HOR.   Indeed? I heard it not. It then draws near the season
        Wherein the spirit held his wont to walk.
        [*A flourish of trumpets, and two pieces go off.*
        What does this mean, my lord?

HAM.   The King doth wake to-night and takes his rouse,
        Keeps wassail, and the swagg'ring up-spring reels,
        And, as he drains his draughts of Rhenish down,
        The kettle-drum and trumpet thus bray out
        The triumph of his pledge.

HOR.   Is it a custom?

HAM.   Ay, marry, is't;
        But to my mind, though I am native here
        And to the manner born, it is a custom
        More honour'd in the breach than the observance.
        This heavy-headed revel east and west
        Makes us traduc'd and tax'd of other nations;
        They clepe us drunkards, and with swinish phrase
        Soil our addition; and, indeed, it takes
        From our achievements, though perform'd at height,

The pith and marrow of our attribute.
So, oft it chances in particular men
That, for some vicious mole of nature in them,
As in their birth, wherein they are not guilty,
Since nature cannot choose his origin;
By the o'ergrowth of some complexion,
Oft breaking down the pales and forts of reason;
Or by some habit that too much o'erleavens
The form of plausive manners—that these men,
Carrying, I say, the stamp of one defect,
Being nature's livery or fortune's star,
His virtues else, be they as pure as grace,
As infinite as man may undergo,
Shall in the general censure take corruption
From that particular fault. The dram of eale
Doth all the noble substance of a doubt
To his own scandal.

ENTER GHOST.

HOR.	Look, my lord, it comes.
HAM.	Angels and ministers of grace defend us!
	Be thou a spirit of health or goblin damn'd,
	Bring with thee airs from heaven or blasts from hell,
	Be thy intents wicked or charitable,
	Thou com'st in such a questionable shape

That I will speak to thee. I'll call thee Hamlet,
King, father, royal Dane. O, answer me!
Let me not burst in ignorance, but tell
Why thy canoniz'd bones, hearsed in death,
Have burst their cerements; why the sepulchre
Wherein we saw thee quietly enurn'd
Hath op'd his ponderous and marble jaws
To cast thee up again. What may this mean
That thou, dead corse, again in complete steel
Revisits thus the glimpses of the moon,
Making night hideous, and we fools of nature
So horridly to shake our disposition
With thoughts beyond the reaches of our souls?
Say, why is this? wherefore? What should we do?   [*Ghost beckons Hamlet.*

HOR.   It beckons you to go away with it,
As if it some impartment did desire
To you alone.

MAR.   Look with what courteous action
It waves you to a more removed ground.
But do not go with it.

HOR.   No, by no means.

HAM.   It will not speak; then I will follow it.

HOR.   Do not, my lord.

HAM.   Why, what should be the fear?
I do not set my life at a pin's fee;
And for my soul, what can it do to that,

	Being a thing immortal as itself?
	It waves me forth again; I'll follow it.
HOR.	What if it tempt you toward the flood, my lord,
	Or to the dreadful summit of the cliff
	That beetles o'er his base into the sea,
	And there assume some other horrible form,
	Which might deprive your sovereignty of reason
	And draw you into madness? Think of it:
	The very place puts toys of desperation,
	Without more motive, into every brain
	That looks so many fathoms to the sea
	And hears it roar beneath.
HAM.	It waves me still.
	Go on; I'll follow thee.
MAR.	You shall not go, my lord.
HAM.	Hold off your hands.
HOR.	Be rul'd; you shall not go.
HAM.	My fate cries out,
	And makes each petty arture in this body
	As hardy as the Nemean lion's nerve.

[*Ghost beckons.*

Still am I call'd. Unhand me, gentlemen.
By heaven, I'll make a ghost of him that lets me.
I say, away! Go on; I'll follow thee.

[*Exeunt Ghost and Hamlet.*

| HOR. | He waxes desperate with imagination. |

MAR.   Let's follow; 'tis not fit thus to obey him.
HOR.   Have after. To what issue will this come?
MAR.   Something is rotten in the state of Denmark.
HOR.   Heaven will direct it.
MAR.   Nay, let's follow him.   [*Exeunt.*

SCENE V

Elsinore. The battlements of the Castle.

ENTER GHOST AND HAMLET.

HAM.   Whither wilt thou lead me?
        Speak, I'll go no further.
GHOST. Mark me.
HAM.   I will.
GHOST. My hour is almost come,
        When I to sulph'rous and tormenting flames
        Must render up myself.
HAM.   Alas, poor ghost!
GHOST. Pity me not, but lend thy serious hearing
        To what I shall unfold.
HAM.   Speak; I am bound to hear.
GHOST. So art thou to revenge, when thou shalt hear.
HAM.   What?
GHOST. I am thy father's spirit,
        Doom'd for a certain term to walk the night,

And for the day confin'd to fast in fires,
Till the foul crimes done in my days of nature
Are burnt and purg'd away. But that I am forbid
To tell the secrets of my prison-house,
I could a tale unfold whose lightest word
Would harrow up thy soul, freeze thy young blood,
Make thy two eyes, like stars, start from their spheres,
Thy knotted and combined locks to part,
And each particular hair to stand an end,
Like quills upon the fretful porpentine.
But this eternal blazon must not be
To ears of flesh and blood. List, list, O, list!
If thou didst ever thy dear father love—

HAM.   O God!

GHOST.   Revenge his foul and most unnatural murder.

HAM.   Murder!

GHOST.   Murder most foul, as in the best it is;
              But this most foul, strange, and unnatural.

HAM.   Haste me to know't, that I, with wings as swift
              As meditation or the thoughts of love,
              May sweep to my revenge.

GHOST.   I find thee apt;
              And duller shouldst thou be than the fat weed
              That roots itself in ease on Lethe wharf,

Wouldst thou not stir in this. Now, Hamlet,
hear:
'Tis given out that, sleeping in my orchard,
A serpent stung me; so the whole ear of
Denmark
Is by a forged process of my death
Rankly abus'd; but know, thou noble youth,
The serpent that did sting thy father's life
Now wears his crown.

HAM.   O my prophetic soul!
My uncle!

GHOST. Ay, that incestuous, that adulterate beast,
With witchcraft of his wits, with traitorous
gifts—
O wicked wit and gifts that have the power
So to seduce!—won to his shameful lust
The will of my most seeming virtuous queen.
O Hamlet, what a falling off was there,
From me, whose love was of that dignity
That it went hand in hand even with the vow
I made to her in marriage; and to decline
Upon a wretch whose natural gifts were poor
To those of mine!
But virtue, as it never will be moved,
Though lewdness court it in a shape of
heaven,
So lust, though to a radiant angel link'd,
Will sate itself in a celestial bed

And prey on garbage.
But soft! methinks I scent the morning air.
Brief let me be. Sleeping within my orchard,
My custom always of the afternoon,
Upon my secure hour thy uncle stole,
With juice of cursed hebona in a vial,
And in the porches of my ears did pour
The leperous distilment; whose effect
Holds such an enmity with blood of man
That swift as quicksilver it courses through
The natural gates and alleys of the body;
And with a sudden vigour it doth posset
And curd, like eager droppings into milk,
The thin and wholesome blood. So did it mine;
And a most instant tetter bark'd about,
Most lazar-like, with vile and loathsome crust,
All my smooth body.
Thus was I, sleeping, by a brother's hand
Of life, of crown, of queen, at once dispatch'd;
Cut off even in the blossoms of my sin,
Unhous'led; disappointed, unanel'd;
No reck'ning made, but sent to my account
With all my imperfections on my head.
O, horrible! O, horrible! most horrible!
If thou hast nature in thee, bear it not;
Let not the royal bed of Denmark be
A couch for luxury and damned incest.

But, howsomever thou pursuest this act,
Taint not thy mind, nor let thy soul contrive
Against thy mother aught; leave her to heaven,
And to those thorns that in her bosom lodge
To prick and sting her. Fare thee well at once.
The glowworm shows the matin to be near,
And gins to pale his uneffectual fire.
Adieu, adieu, adieu! Remember me.   [*Exit.*

HAM.   O all you host of heaven! O earth! What else?
And shall I couple hell? O, fie! Hold, hold, my heart;
And you, my sinews, grow not intant old,
But bear me stiffly up. Remember thee!
Ay, thou poor ghost, whiles memory holds a seat
In this distracted globe. Remember thee!
Yea, from the table of my memory
I'll wipe away all trivial fond records,
All saws of books, all forms, all pressures past,
That youth and observation copied there,
And thy commandment all alone shall live
Within the book and volume of my brain,
Unmix'd with baser matter. Yes, by heaven!
O most pernicious woman!
O villain, villain, smiling, damned villain!
My tables—meet it is I set it down
That one may smile, and smile, and be a villain;

At least I am sure it may be so in Denmark.
                                    [*Writing*.
So, uncle, there you are. Now to my word:
It is 'Adieu, adieu! Remember me'.
I have sworn't.

HOR. [*Within*] My lord, my lord!

ENTER HORATIO AND MARCELLUS.

MAR.   Lord Hamlet!
HOR.   Heavens secure him!
HAM.   So be it!
MAR.   Illo, ho, ho, my lord!
HAM.   Hillo, ho, ho, boy! Come, bird, come.
MAR.   How is't, my noble lord?
HOR.   What news, my lord?
HAM.   O, wonderful!
HOR.   Good my lord, tell it.
HAM.   No; you will reveal it.
HOR.   Not I, my lord, by heaven!
MAR.   Nor I, my lord.
HAM.   How say you, then; would heart of man once
       think it?
       But you'll be secret?
BOTH. Ay, by heaven, my lord!
HAM.   There's never a villain dwelling in all Denmark
       But he's an arrant knave.
HOR.   There needs no ghost, my lord, come from
       the grave
       To tell us this.

HAM.   Why, right; you are in the right;
         And so, without more circumstance at all,
         I hold it fit that we shake hands and part;
         You, as your business and desire shall point you—
         For every man hath business and desire,
         Such as it is; and for my own poor part,
         Look you, I will go pray.

HOR.   These are but wild and whirling words, my lord.

HAM.   I am sorry they offend you, heartily;
         Yes, faith, heartily.

HOR.   There's no offence, my lord.

HAM.   Yes, by Saint Patrick, but there is, Horatio,
         And much offence too. Touching this vision here—
         It is an honest ghost, that let me tell you.
         For your desire to know what is between us,
         O'ermaster't as you may. And now, good friends,
         As you are friends, scholars, and soldiers,
         Give me one poor request.

HOR.   What is't, my lord? We will.

HAM.   Never make known what you have seen to-night.

BOTH.   My lord, we will not.

HAM.   Nay, but swear't.

HOR.   In faith,

	My lord, not I.
MAR.	Nor I, my lord, in faith.
HAM.	Upon my sword.
MAR.	We have sworn, my lord, already.
HAM.	Indeed, upon my sword, indeed.
GHOST.	[*Cries under the stage*] Swear.
HAM.	Ha, ha, boy! say'st thou so? Art thou there, truepenny?
	Come on. You hear this fellow in the cellarage:
	Consent to swear.
HOR.	Propose the oath, my lord.
HAM.	Never to speak of this that you have seen,
	Swear by my sword.
GHOST.	[*Beneath*] Swear.
HAM.	Hic et ubique? Then we'll shift our ground.
	Come hither, gentlemen,
	And lay your hands again upon my sword.
	Swear by my sword
	Never to speak of this that you have heard.
GHOST.	[*Beneath*] Swear, by his sword.
HAM.	Well said, old mole! Canst work i' th' earth so fast?
	A worthy pioneer! Once more remove, good friends.
HOR.	O day and night, but this is wondrous strange!
HAM.	And therefore as a stranger give it welcome.
	There are more things in heaven and earth,

Horatio,
Than are dreamt of in your philosophy.
But come.
Here, as before, never, so help you mercy,
How strange or odd some'er I bear myself—
As I perchance hereafter shall think meet
To put an antic disposition on—
That you, at such times, seeing me, never
shall,
With arms encumb'red thus, or this head-
shake,
Or by pronouncing of some doubtful phrase,
As 'Well, well, we know' or 'We could, an if
we would'
Or 'If we list to speak' or 'There be, an if
they might'
Or such ambiguous giving out, to note
That you know aught of me—this do swear,
So grace and mercy at your most need help
you.

GHOST. [*Beneath*] Swear.

HAM.   Rest, rest, perturbed spirit! So, gentlemen,
With all my love I do commend me to you;
And what so poor a man as Hamlet is
May do t'express his love and friending to
you,
God willing, shall not lack. Let us go in
together;

And still your fingers on your lips, I pray.
The time is out of joint. O cursed spite,
That ever I was born to set it right!
Nay, come, let's go together.   [*Exeunt.*

ACT II SCENE I

Elsinore. The house of Polonius.

ENTER POLONIUS AND REYNALDO.

POL.   Give him this money and these notes,
           Reynaldo.

REY.   I will, my lord.

POL.   You shall do marvellous wisely, good
           Reynaldo,
           Before you visit him, to make inquire
           Of his behaviour.

REY.   My lord, I did intend it.

POL.   Marry, well said; very well said.
           Look you, sir,
           Enquire me first what Danskers are in Paris;
           And how, and who, what means, and where

they keep,
What company, at what expense; and finding
By this encompassment and drift of question
That they do know my son, come you more nearer
Than your particular demands will touch it.
Take you, as 'twere, some distant knowledge of him;
As thus : 'I know his father and his friends,
And in part him'. Do you mark this, Reynaldo?

REY.   Ay, very well, my lord.

POL.   'And in part him—but' you may say 'not well;
But if't be he I mean, he's very wild;
Addicted so and so'; and there put on him
What forgeries you please; marry, none so rank
As may dishonour him; take heed of that;
But, sir, such wanton, wild, and usual slips
As are companions noted and most known
To youth and liberty.

REY.   As gaming, my Lord.

POL.   Ay, or drinking, fencing, swearing, quarrelling,
Drabbing—you may go so far.

REY.   My lord, that would dishonour him.

POL.   Faith, no; as you may season it in the charge.
You must not put another scandal on him,
That he is open to incontinency;
That's not my meaning. But breathe his faults
so quaintly

That they may seem the taints of liberty;
The flash and outbreak of a fiery mind,
A savageness in unreclaimed blood,
Of general assault.

REY.   But, my good lord—
POL.   Wherefore should you do this?
REY.   Ay, my lord,
I would know that.
POL.   Marry, sir, here's my drift,
And I believe it is a fetch of warrant:
You laying these slight sullies on my son,
As 'twere a thing a little soil'd wi' th' working,
Mark you,
Your party in converse, him you would sound,
Having ever seen in the prenominate crimes
The youth you breathe of guilty, be assur'd
He closes with you in this consequence—
'Good sir' or so, or 'friend' or 'gentleman'
According to the phrase or the addition
Of man and country.
REY.   Very good, my lord.
POL.   And then, sir, does 'a this—'a does—
What was I about to say? By the mass,
I was about to say something; where did I
leave?
REY.   At 'closes in the consequence', at 'friend or
so' and 'gentleman'.
POL.   At 'closes in the consequence '—ay, marry,
He closes thus : 'I know the gentleman;

I saw him yesterday, or t'other day,
Or then, or then; with such, or such; and, as
you say,
There was 'a gaming; there o'ertook in's rouse;
There falling out at tennis'; or perchance
'I saw him enter such a house of sale'
Videlicet, a brothel, or so forth. See you now
Your bait of falsehood take this carp of truth;
And thus do we of wisdom and of reach,
With windlasses and with assays of bias,
By indirections find directions out;
So, by my former lecture and advice,
Shall you my son. You have me, have you
not?

REY.   My lord, I have.
POL.   God buy ye; fare ye well.
REY.   Good my lord!
POL.   Observe his inclination in yourself.
REY.   I shall, my lord.
POL.   And let him ply his music.
REY.   Well, my lord.
POL.   Farewell!   [*Exit Reynaldo.*

ENTER OPHELIA.

How now, Ophelia! What's the matter?
OPH.   O my lord, my lord, I have been so affrighted!
POL.   With what, i' th' name of God?
OPH.   My lord, as I was sewing in my closet,
Lord Hamlet, with his doublet all unbrac'd,

No hat upon his head, his stockings fouled,
Ungart'red and down-gyved to his ankle;
Pale as his shirt, his knees knocking each other,
And with a look so piteous in purport
As if he had been loosed out of hell
To speak of horrors—he comes before me.

POL. Mad for thy love?

OPH. My lord, I do not know,
But truly I do fear it.

POL. What said he?

OPH. He took me by the wrist, and held me hard;
Then goes he to the length of all his arm,
And, with his other hand thus o'er his brow,
He falls to such perusal of my face
As 'a would draw it. Long stay'd he so.
At last, a little shaking of mine arm,
And thrice his head thus waving up and down,
He rais'd a sigh so piteous and profound
As it did seem to shatter all his bulk
And end his being. That done, he lets me go,
And, with his head over his shoulder turn'd,
He seem'd to find his way without his eyes;
For out adoors he went without their helps
And to the last bended their light on me.

POL. Come, go with me. I will go seek the King.
This is the very ecstasy of love,
Whose violent property fordoes itself,
And leads the will to desperate undertakings
As oft as any passion under heaven

That does afflict our natures. I am sorry—
What, have you given him any hard words of
late?

OPH. No, my good lord; but, as you did command,
I did repel his letters, and denied
His access to me.

POL. That hath made him mad.
I am sorry that with better heed and judgment
I had not quoted him. I fear'd he did but trifle,
And meant to wreck thee; but beshrew my
jealousy!
By heaven, it is as proper to our age
To cast beyond ourselves in our opinions
As it is common for the younger sort
To lack discretion. Come, go we to the King.
This must be known; which, being kept
close, might move
More grief to hide than hate to utter love.
Come.   [*Exeunt.*

SCENE II

Elsinore. The Castle.

FLOURISH. ENTER KING, QUEEN, ROSENCRANTZ,
GUILDENSTERN, AND ATTENDANTS.

KING. Welcome, dear Rosencrantz and Guildenstern!

Moreover that we much did long to see you,
The need we have to use you did provoke
Our hasty sending. Something have you heard
Of Hamlet's transformation; so I call it,
Sith nor th' exterior nor the inward man
Resembles that it was. What it should be,
More than his father's death, that thus hath
put him
So much from th' understanding of himself,
I cannot deem of. I entreat you both
That, being of so young days brought up with
him,
And sith so neighboured to his youth and
haviour,
That you vouchsafe your rest here in our court
Some little time; so by your companies
To draw him on to pleasures, and to gather,
So much as from occasion you may glean,
Whether aught to us unknown afflicts him
thus
That, open'd, lies within our remedy.

QUEEN. Good gentlemen, he hath much talk'd of you;
And sure I am two men there is not living
To whom he more adheres. If it will please
you
To show us so much gentry and good will
As to expend your time with us awhile
For the supply and profit of our hope,
Your visitation shall receive such thanks

As fits a king's remembrance.

ROS.   Both your Majesties
Might, by the sovereign power you have of us,
Put your dread pleasures more into command
Than to entreaty.

GUIL.   But we both obey,
And here give up ourselves, in the full bent,
To lay our service freely at your feet,
To be commanded.

KING.   Thanks, Rosencrantz and gentle Guildenstern.

QUEEN.   Thanks, Guildenstern and gentle Rosencrantz.
And I beseech you instantly to visit
My too much changed son. Go, some of you,
And bring these gentlemen where Hamlet is.

GUIL.   Heavens make our presence and our practices
Pleasant and helpful to him!

QUEEN.   Aye amen!

*[Exeunt Rosencrantz, Guildenstern,
and some Attendants.*

ENTER POLONIUS.

POL.   Th' ambassadors from Norway, my good lord,
Are joyfully return'd.

KING.   Thou still hast been the father of good news.

POL.   Have I, my lord? I assure you, my good liege,
I hold my duty, as I hold my soul,
Both to my God and to my gracious King;

	And I do think—or else this brain of mine

And I do think—or else this brain of mine
Hunts not the trail of policy so sure
As it hath us'd to do—that I have found
The very cause of Hamlet's lunacy.

KING.   O, speak of that; that do I long to hear.

POL.   Give first admittance to th' ambassadors;
My news shall be the fruit to that great feast.

KING.   Thyself do grace to them, and bring them in.
                              [*Exit Polonius.*
He tells me, my dear Gertrude, he hath found
The head and source of all your son's
distemper.

QUEEN.. I doubt it is no other but the main,
His father's death and our o'erhasty marriage.

KING.   Well, we shall sift him.

RE-ENTER POLONIUS, WITH VOLTEMAND AND
CORNELIUS.

Welcome, my good friends!
Say, Voltemand, what from our brother
Norway?

VOLT.   Most fair return of greetings and desires.
Upon our first, he sent out to suppress
His nephew's levies; which to him appear'd
To be a preparation 'gainst the Polack;
But, better look'd into, he truly found
It was against your Highness. Whereat griev'd,
That so his sickness, age, and impotence,

Was falsely borne in hand, sends out arrests
On Fortinbras; which he, in brief, obeys;
Receives rebuke from Norway; and, in fine,
Makes vow before his uncle never more
To give th' assay of arms against your Majesty.
Whereon old Norway, overcome with joy,
Gives him threescore thousand crowns in
annual fee,
And his commission to employ those soldiers,
So leied as before, against the Polack;
With an entreaty, herein further shown,

                     [*Gives a paper.*

That it might please you to give quiet pass
Through your dominions for this enterprise,
On such regards of safety and allowance
As therein are set down.

KING.   It likes us well;
And at our more considered time we'll read,
Answer, and think upon this business.
Meantime we thank you for your well-took
labour.
Go to your rest; at night we'll feast together.
Most welcome home!

        [*Exeunt Ambassadors and Attendants.*

POL.   This business is well ended.
My liege, and madam, to expostulate
What majesty should be, what duty is,
Why day is day, night night, and time is time,

Were nothing, but to waste night, day, and
time.
Therefore, since brevity is the soul of wit,
And tediousness the limbs and outward
flourishes,
I will be brief. Your noble son is mad.
Mad call I it; for, to define true madness,
What is't but to be nothing else but mad?
But let that go.

QUEEN. More matter with less art.

POL. Madam, I swear I use no art at all.
That he's mad, 'tis true: 'tis true 'tis pity;
And pity 'tis 'tis true. A foolish figure!
But farewell it, for I will use no art.
Mad let us grant him, then; and now remains
That we find out the cause of this effect;
Or rather say the cause of this defect,
For this effect defective comes by cause.
Thus it remains, and the remainder thus.
Perpend.
I have a daughter—have while she is mine—
Who in her duty and obedience, mark,
Hath given me this. Now gather, and surmise.
                                    [*Reads.*
'To the celestial, and my soul's idol, the most
beautified Ophelia.' That's an ill phrase, a vile
phrase; 'beautified' is a vile phrase. But you
shall hear. Thus: [*Reads.*

'In her excellent white bosom, these, &c.'

QUEEN. Came this from Hamlet to her?

POL. Good madam, stay awhile; I will be faithful.

[*Reads.*

'Doubt thou the stars are fire;
Doubt that the sun doth move;
Doubt truth to be a liar;
But never doubt I love.
O dear Ophelia, I am ill at these numbers.
I have not art to reckon my groans; but that I
love thee best, O most best, believe it. Adieu.
Thine evermore, most dear lady, whilst this
machine is to him,   HAMLET.'
This, in obedience,hath my daughter shown
me;
And more above, hath his solicitings,
As they fell out by time, by means, and place,
All given to mine eat.

KING. But how hath she
Receiv'd his love?

POL. What do you think of me?

KING. As of a man faithful and honourable.

POL. I would fain prove so. But what might you
think,
When I had seen this hot love on the wing,
As I perceiv'd it, I must tell you that,
Before my daughter told me—what might
you,

Or my dear Majesty your queen here, think,
If I had play'd the desk or table-book;
Or given my heart a winking, mute and
dumb;
Or look'd upon this love with idle sight—
What might you think? No, I went round to
work,
And my young mistress thus I did bespeak:
'Lord Hamet is a prince out of thy star;
This must not be'. And then I prescripts gave
her,
That she should lock herself from his resort,
Admit no messengers, receive no tokens.
Which done, she took the fruits of my advice;
And he repelled, a short tale to make,
Fell into a sadness, then into a fast,
Thence to a watch, thence into a weakness,
Thence to a lightness, and, by this declension,
Into the madness wherein now he raves
And all we mourn for.

KING.   Do you think 'tis this?
QUEEN. It may be, very like.
POL.   Hath there been such a time—I would fain
        know that—
        That I have positively said ' 'Tis so',
        When it prov'd otherwise?
KING.   Not that I know.
POL.   Take this from this, if this be otherwise.

	If circumstances lead me, I will find
	Where truth is hid, though it were hid indeed
	Within the centre.
KING.	How may we try it further?
POL.	You know sometimes he walks four hours together,
	Here in the lobby.
QUEEN.	So he does, indeed.
POL.	At such a time I'll loose my daughter to him.
	Be you and I behind an arras then;
	Mark the encounter: if he love her not,
	And be not from his reason fall'n thereon,
	Let me be no assistant for a state,
	But keep a farm and carters.
KING.	We will try it.

ENTER HAMLET, READING ON A BOOK.

QUEEN.	But look where sadly the poor wretch comes reading.
POL.	Away, I do beseech you, both away:
	I'll board him presently. O, give me leave.
	[*Exeunt King and Queen.*
	How does my good Lord Hamlet?
HAM.	Well, God-a-mercy.
POL.	Do you know me, my lord?
HAM.	Excellent well; you are a fishmonger.
POL.	Not I, my lord.
HAM.	Then I would you were so honest a man.

POL.   Honest, my lord!

HAM.   Ay, sir; to be honest, as this world goes, is to
          be one man pick'd out of ten thousand.

POL.   That's very true, my lord.

HAM.   For if the sun breed maggots in a dead dog,
          being a good kissing carrion—Have you a
          daughter?

POL.   I have, my lord.

HAM.   Let her not walk i' th' sun. Conception is a
          blessing. But as your daughter may conceive—
          friend, look to't.

POL.   How say you by that? [*Aside*] Still harping
          on my daughter. Yet he knew me not at first;
          'a said I was a fishmonger. 'A is far gone, far
          gone. And truly in my youth I suff'red much
          extremity for love. Very near this. I'll speak
          to him again.—What do you read, my lord?

HAM.   Words, words, words.

POL.   What is the matter, my lord?

HAM.   Between who?

POL.   I mean, the matter that you read, my lord.

HAM.   Slanders, sir; for the satirical rogue says here
          that old men have grey beards; that their faces
          are wrinkled; their eyes purging thick amber
          and plumtree gum; and that they have a
          plentiful lack of wit, together with most weak
          hams—all which, sir, though I most
          powerfully and potently believe, yet I hold it
          not honesty to have it thus set down; for you

yourself, sir, shall grow old as I am, if, like a
crab, you could go backward.

POL.   [*Aside*] Though this be madness, yet there is
         method in't.—Will you walk out of the air,
         my lord?

HAM.   Into my grave?

POL.   Indeed, that's out of the air. [*Aside*]
         How pregnant sometimes his replies are! a
         happiness that often madness hits on, which
         reason and sanity could not so prosperously
         be delivered of. I will leave him, and suddenly
         contrive the means of meeting between him
         and my daughter.
         —My lord, I will take my leave of you.

HAM.   You cannot, sir, take from the anything that I
         will more willingly part withal—except my
         life, except my life, except my life.

ENTER ROSENCRANTZ AND GUILDENSTERN.

POL.   Fare you well, my lord.

HAM.   These tedious old fools!

POL.   You go to seek the Lord Hamlet; there he is.

ROS.   [*To Polonius*] God save you, sir!

                                    [*Exit Polonius.*

GUIL.   My honour'd lord!

ROS.   My most dear lord!

HAM.   My excellent good friends! How dost thou,
         Guildenstern? Ah, Rosencrantz! Good lads,
         how do you both?

ROS.   As the indifferent children of the earth.

GUIL.   Happy in that we are not over happy;
        On fortune's cap we are not the very button.

HAM.   Nor the soles of her shoe?

ROS.   Neither, my lord.

HAM.   Then you live about her waist, or in the middle
        of her favours?

GUIL.   Faith, her privates we.

HAM.   In the secret parts of Fortune? O, most true;
        she is a strumpet. What news?

ROS.   None, my lord, but that the world's grown
        honest.

HAM.   Then is doomsday near. But your news is not
        true. Let me question more in particular.
        What have you, my good friends, deserved at
        the hands of Fortune, that she sends you to
        prison hither?

GUIL.   Prison, my lord!

HAM.   Denmark's a prison.

ROS.   Then is the world one.

HAM.   A goodly one; in which there are many
        confines, wards, and dungeons, Denmark
        being one o' th' worst.

ROS.   We think not so, my lord.

HAM.   Why, then, 'tis none to you; for there is
        nothing either good or bad, but thinking
        makes it so. To me it is a prison.

ROS.   Why, then your ambition makes it one; 'tis
        too narrow for your mind.

HAM.   O God, I could be bounded in a nutshell and
        count myself a king of infinite space, were it
        not that I have bad dreams.

GUIL.   Which dreams indeed are ambition; for the
        very substance of the ambitious is merely the
        shadow of a dream.

HAM.   A dream itself is but a shadow.

ROS.   Truly, and I hold ambition of so airy and light
        a quality that it is but a shadow's shadow.

HAM.   Then are our beggars bodies, and our
        monarchs and outstretch'd heroes the beggars'
        shadows. Shall we to th' court? for, by my
        fay, I cannot reason.

BOTH.   We'll wait upon you.

HAM.   No such matter. I will not sort you with the
        rest of my servants; for, to speak to you like
        an honest man, I am most dreadfully
        attended. But, in the beaten way of
        friendship, what make you at Elsinore?

RAS.   To visit you, my lord; no other occasion.

HAM.   Beggar that I am, I am even poor in thanks;
        but I thank you; and sure, dear friends, my
        thanks are too dear a half-penny. Were you
        not sent for? Is it your own inclining? Is it a
        free visitation? Come, come, deal justly with
        me. Come, come; nay, speak.

GUIL.   What should we say, my lord?

HAM.   Why any thing. But to th' purpose: you were

	sent for; and there is a kind of confession in your looks, which your modesties have not craft enough to colour; I know the good King and Queen have sent for you.
ROS.	To what end, my lord?
HAM.	That you must teach me. But let me conjure you by the rights of our fellowship, by the consonancy of our youth, by the obligation of our ever-preserved love, and by what more dear a better proposer can charge you withal, be even and direct with me, whether you were sent for or no?
ROS.	[*Aside to Guildenstern*] What say you?
HAM.	[*Aside*] Nay, then, I have an eye of you.—If you love me, hold not off.
GUIL.	My lord, we were sent for.
HAM.	I will tell you why; so shall my anticipation prevent your discovery, and your secrecy to the King and Queen moult no feather. I have of late—but wherefore I know not—lost all my mirth, forgone all custom of exercises; and indeed it goes so heavily with my disposition that this goodly frame, the earth, seems to me a sterile promontory; this most excellent canopy the air, look you, this brave o'erhanging firmament, this majestical roof fretted with golden fire—why, it appeareth no other thing to me than a foul and pestilent

congregation of vapours. What a piece of work is a man! How noble in reason! how infinite in faculties! in form and moving, how express and admirable! in action, how like an angel! in apprehension, how like a god! the beauty of the world! the paragon of animals! And yet, to me, what is this quintessence of dust? Man delights not me—no, nor woman neither, though by your smiling you seem to say so.

ROS.   My lord, there was no such stuff in my thoughts.

HAM.   Why did ye laugh, then, when I said 'man delights not me'?

ROS.   To think, my lord, if you delight not in man, what lenten entertainment the players shall receive from you. We coted them on the way; and hither are they coming to offer you service.

HAM.   He that plays the king shall be welcome—his Majesty shall have tribute on me; the adventurous knight shall use his foil and target; the lover shall not sigh gratis; the humorous man shall end his part in peace; the clown shall make those laugh whose lungs are tickle a' th' sere; and the lady shall say her mind freely, or the blank verse shall halt for't. What players are they?

ROS.   Even those you were wont to take such
         delight in—the tragedians of the city.

HAM.   How chances it they travel? Their residence,
         both in reputation and profit, was better both
         ways.

ROS.   I think their inhibition comes by the means
         of the late innovation.

HAM.   Do they hold the same estimation they did
         when I was in the city? Are they so followed?

ROS.   No, indeed, are they not.

HAM.   How comes it? Do they grow rusty?

ROS.   Nay, their endeavour keeps in the wonted
         pace; but there is, sir, an eyrie of children,
         little eyases, that cry out on the top of
         question, and are most tyrannically clapp'd
         for't. These are now the fashion, and so
         berattle the common stages—so they call
         them—that many wearing rapiers are afraid
         of goose quills and dare scarce come thither.

HAM.   What, are they children? Who maintains 'em?
         How are they escoted? Will they pursue the
         quality no longer than they can sing? Will
         they not say afterwards, if they should grow
         themselves to common players—as it is most
         like, if their means are no better—their writers
         do them wrong to make them exclaim against
         their own succession?

ROS.   Faith, there has been much to-do on both
         sides; and the nation holds it no sin to tarre

	them to controversy. There was for a while no money bid for argument, unless the poet and the player went to cuffs in the question.
HAM.	Is't possible?
GUIL.	O, there has been much throwing about of brains.
HAM.	Do the boys carry it away?
ROS.	Ay, that they do, my lord— Hercules and his load too.
HAM.	It is not very strange; for my uncle is King of Denmark, and those that would make mows at him while my father lived give twenty, forty, fifty, a hundred ducats apiece for his picture in little. 'Sblood, there is something in this more than natural, if philosophy could find it out. [*A flourish.*
GUIL.	There are the players.
HAM.	Gentlemen, you are welcome to Elsinore. Your hands, come then; th' appurtenance of welcome is fashion and ceremony. Let me comply with you in this garb; lest my extent to the players, which, I tell you, must show fairly outwards, should more appear like entertainment than yours. You are welcome. But my uncle-father and aunt-mother are deceived.
GUIL.	In what, my dear lord?
HAM.	I am but mad north-north-west; when the

wind is southerly I know a hawk from a handsaw.

RE-ENTER POLONIUS.

POL.   Well be with you, gentlemen!

HAM.   Hark you, Guildenstern, and you too—at each ear a hearer: that great baby you see there is not yet out of his swaddling clouts.

ROS.   Happily he is the second time come to them; for they say an old man is twice a child.

HAM.   I will prophesy he comes to tell me of the players; mark it. You say right, sir: a Monday morning; 'twas then indeed.

POL.   My lord, I have news to tell you.

HAM.   My lord, I have news to tell you. When Roscius was an actor in Rome—

POL.   The actors are come hither, my lord.

HAM.   Buzz, buzz!

POL.   Upon my honour—

HAM.   Then came each actor on his ass—

POL.   The best actors in the world, either for tragedy, comedy, history, pastoral, pastoral-comical, historical-pastoral, tragical-historical, tragical-comical-historical-pastoral, scene individable, or poem unlimited. Seneca cannot be too heavy nor Plautus too light. For the law of writ and the liberty, these are the only men.

HAM.   O Jephthah, judge of Israel, what a treasure hadst thou!

POL. What a treasure had he, my lord?

HAM Why—
'One fair daughter, and no more,
The which he loved passing well'.

POL. [*Aside*] Still on my daughter.

HAM. Am I not i' th' right, old Jephthah?

POL. If you call me Jephthah, my lord, I have a
daughter that I love passing well.

HAM. Nay, that follows not.

POL. What follows then, my lord?

HAM. Why—
'As by lot, God wot'
and then, you know,
'It came to pass, as most like it was'.
The first row of the pious chanson will show
you more; for look where my abridgement
comes.

ENTER THE PLAYERS.

You are welcome, masters; welcome, all.—I
am glad to see thee well.—Welcome, good
friends.—O, my old friend! Why thy face is
valanc'd since I saw thee last; com'st thou to
beard me in Denmark?—What, my young
lady and mistress! By'r lady, your ladyship is
nearer to heaven than when I saw you last by
the altitude of a chopine. Pray God, your.
voice, like a piece of uncurrent gold, be not

crack'd within the ring.—Masters, you are all welcome. We'll e'en to't like French falconers, fly at anything we see. We'll have a speech straight. Come, give us a taste of your quality; come, a passionate speech.

1 PLAY.   What speech, my good lord?

HAM.   I heard thee speak me a speech once, but it was never acted; or, if it was, not above once; for the play, I remember, pleas'd not the million; 'twas caviary to the general. But it was—as I received it, and others whose judgments in such matters cried in the top of mine—an excellent play, well digested in the scenes, set down with as much modesty as cunning. I remember one said there were no sallets in the lines to make the matter savoury, nor no matter in the phrase that might indict the author of affectation; but call'd it an honest method, as wholesome as sweet, and by very much more handsome than fine. One speech in it I chiefly lov'd : 'twas Æneas' tale to Dido; and thereabout of it especially where he speaks of Priam's slaughter. If it live in your memory, begin at this line—let me see, let me see :
'The rugged Pyrrhus, like th' Hyrcanian beast,'
'Tis not so; it begins with Pyrrhus.
'The rugged Pyrrhus, he whose sable arms,

Black as his purpose, did the night resemble
When he lay couched in the ominous horse,
Hath now this dread and black complexion smear'd
With heraldry more dismal; head to foot
Now is he total gules, horridly trick'd
With blood of fathers, mothers, daughters, sons,
Bak'd and impasted with the parching streets,
That lend a tyrannous and damned light
To their lord's murder. Roasted in wrath and fire,
And thus o'er-sized with coagulate gore,
With eyes like carbuncles, the hellish Pyrrhus
Old grandsire Priam seeks.'
So proceed you.

POL.   Fore God, my lord, well spoken, with good accent and good discretion.

1 PLAY.   'Anon he finds him
Striking too short at Greeks; his antique sword,
Rebellious to his arm, lies where it falls,
Repugnant to command. Unequal match'd,
Pyrrhus at Priam drives, in rage strikes wide;
But with the whiff and wind of his fell sword
Th' unnerved father, falls. Then senseless Ilium,
Seeming to feel this blow, with flaming top

Stoops to his base, and with a hideous crash
Takes prisoner Pyrrhus' ear. For, lo! his sword,
Which was declining on the milky head
Of reverend Priam, seem'd i' th' air to stick.
So, as a painted tyrant, Pyrrhus stood
And, like a neutral to his will and matter,
Did nothing.
But as we often see, against some storm,
A silence in the heavens, the rack stand still,
The bold winds speechless, and the orb below
As hush as death, anon the dreadful thunder
Doth rend the region; so, after Pyrrhus' pause,
A roused vengeance sets him new a-work;
And never did the Cyclops' hammers fall
On Mars's armour, forg'd for proof eterne,
With less remorse than Pyrrhus' bleeding
sword
Now falls on Priam.
Out, out, thou strumpet, Fortune! All you
gods,
In general synod, take away her power;
Break all the spokes and fellies from her
wheel,
And bowl the round nave down the hill of
heaven,
As low as to the fiends.'

POL.   This is too long.

HAM.   It shall to the barber's, with your beard.

Prithee say on. He's for a jig, or a tale of
bawdry, or he sleeps. Say on; come to Hecuba.

1 PLAY.   'But who, ah, who had seen the mobled
          queen—'

HAM.   'The mobled queen'?

POL.   That's good; 'mobled queen' is good.

1 PLAY.   'Run barefoot up and down, threat'ning the
          flames
          With bisson rheum; a clout upon that head
          Where late the diadem stood, and for a robe,
          About her lank and all o'er-teemed loins,
          A blanket, in the alarm of fear caught up—
          Who this had seen, with tongue in venom
          steep'd,
          'Gainst Fortune's state would treason have
          pronounc'd.
          But if the gods themselves did see her then,
          When she saw Pyrrhus make malicious sport
          In mincing with his sword her husband's
          limbs,
          The instant burst of clamour that she made—
          Unless things mortal move them not at all—
          Would have made milch the burning eyes of
          heaven,
          And passion in the gods.'

POL.   Look whe'er he has not turn'd his colour, and
          has tears in 's eyes. Prithee no more.

HAM.   'Tis well; I'll have thee speak out the rest of

this soon.—Good my lord, will you see the players well bestowed? Do you hear : let them be well used; for they are the abstract and brief chronicles of the time; after your death you were better have a bad epitaph than their ill report while you live.

POL. My lord, I will use them according to their desert.

HAM. God's bodykins, man, much better. Use every man after his desert, and who shall scape whipping? Use them after your own honour and dignity: the less they deserve, the more merit is in your bounty. Take them in.

POL. Come, sirs.

HAM. Follow him, friends. We'll hear a play to-morrow. Dost thou hear me, old friend; can you play 'The Murder of Gonzago'?

1 PLAY. Ay, my lord.

HAM. We'll ha't to-morrow night. You could, for a need, study a speech of some dozen or sixteen lines which I would set down and insert in't, could you not?

1 PLAY. Ay, my lord.

HAM. Very well. Follow that lord; and look you mock him not. [*Exeunt Polonius and Players*] My good friends, I'll leave you till night. You are welcome to Elsinore.

ROS. Good my lord!

[*Exeunt Rosencrantz and Guildenstern.*

HAM. Ay, so God buy to you! Now I am alone.
O, what a rogue and peasant slave am I!
Is it not monstrous that this player here,
But in a fiction, in a dream of passion,
Could force his soul so to his own conceit
That from her working all his visage wann'd;
Tears in his eyes, distraction in's aspect,
A broken voice, and his whole function suiting
With forms to his conceit? And all for
nothing!
For Hecuba!
What's Hecuba to him or he to Hecuba,
That he should weep for her? What would
he do,
Had he the motive and the cue for passion
That I have? He would drown the stage with
tears,
And cleave the general ear with horrid speech;
Make mad the guilty, and appal the free,
Confound the ignorant, and amaze indeed
The very faculties of eyes and ears.
Yet I,
A dull and muddy-mettl'd rascal, peak,
Like John-a-dreams, unpregnant of my cause,
And can say nothing; no, not for a king
Upon whose property and most dear life
A damn'd defeat was made. Am I a coward?
You calls me villain, breaks my pate across,

Plucks off my beard and blows it in my face,
Tweaks me by the nose, gives me the lie i' th'
throat
As deep as to the lungs? Who does me this?
Ha!
'Swounds, I should take it; for it cannot be
But I am pigeon-liver'd and lack gall
To make oppression bitter, or ere this
I should 'a fatted all the region kites
With this slave's offal. Bloody, bawdy villain!
Remorseless, treacherous, lecherous, kindless
villain!
O, vengeance!
Why, what an ass am I! This is most brave,
That I, the son of a dear father murder'd,
Prompted to my revenge by heaven and hell,
Must, like a whore, unpack my heart with
words,
And fall a-cursing like a very drab,
A scullion! Fie upon't! foh!
About, my brains. Hum—I have heard
That guilty creatures, sitting at a play,
Have by the very cunning of the scene
Been struck so to the soul that presently
They have proclaim'd their malefactions;
For murder, though it have no tongue, will
speak
With most miraculous organ. I'll have these

players
Play something like the murder of my father
Before mine uncle. I'll observe his looks;
I'll tent him to the quick. If 'a do blench,
I know my course. The spirit that I have seen
May be a devil; and the devil hath power
T' assume a pleasing shape; yea, and perhaps
Out of my weakness and my melancholy,
As he is very potent with such spirits,
Abuses me to damn me. I'll have grounds
More relative than this. The play's the thing
Wherein I'll catch the conscience of the King.
                                        [*Exit.*

ACT III SCENE I

Elsinore. The Castle.

ENTER KING, QUEEN, POLONIUS, OPHELIA,
ROSENCRANTZ, AND GUILDENSTERN.

KING.   And can you by no drift of conference
Get from him why he puts on this confusion,
Grating so harshly all his days of quiet
With turbulent and dangerous lunacy?

ROS.   He does confess he feels himself distracted,
But from what cause 'a will by no means
speak.

GUIL.   Nor do we find him forward to be sounded;
But, with a crafty madness, keeps aloof
When we would bring him on to some
confession

Of his true state.

QUEEN. Did he receive you well?

ROS. Most like a gentleman.

GUIL. But with much forcing of his disposition.

ROS. Niggard of question; but of our demands
Most free in his reply.

QUEEN. Did you assay him
To any pastime?

ROS. Madam, it so fell out that certain players
We o'er-raught on the way. Of these we told
him;
And there did seem in him a kind of joy
To hear of it. They are here about the court,
And, as I think, they have already order
This night to play before him.

POL. 'Tis most true;
And he beseech'd me to entreat your Majesties
To hear and see the matter.

KING. With all my heart; and it doth much content
me
To hear him so inclin'd.
Good gentlemen, give him a further edge,
And drive his purpose into these delights.

ROS. We shall, my lord.
              [*Exeunt Rosencrantz and Guildenstern.*

KING. Sweet Gertrude, leave us too;
For we have closely sent for Hamlet hither,
That he, as 'twere by accident, may here
Affront Ophelia.

Her father and myself—lawful espials—
Will so bestow ourselves that, seeing unseen,
We may of their encounter frankly judge,
And gather by him, as he is behav'd,
If't be th' affliction of his love or no
That thus he suffers for.

QUEEN.   I shall obey you;
And for your part, Ophelia, I do wish
That your good beauties be the happy cause
Of Hamlet's wildness; so shall I hope your
virtues
Will bring him to his wonted way again,
To both your honours.

OPH.   Madam, I wish it may.   [*Exit Queen.*

POL.   Ophelia, walk you here.—Gracious, so please
you,
We will bestow ourselves.—Read on this
book;
That show of such an exercise may colour
Your loneliness.—We are oft to blame in this:
'Tis too much prov'd, that with devotion's
visage
And pious action we do sugar o'er
The devil himself.

KING.   [*Aside*] O, 'tis too true!
How smart a lash that speech doth give my
conscience!
The harlot's cheek, beautied with plast'ring
art,

Is not more ugly to the thing that helps it
Then is my deed to my most painted word.
O heavy burden!

POL.   I hear him coming; let's withdraw, my lord.
                   [*Exeunt King and Polonius.*

ENTER HAMLET.

HAM.   To be, or not to be—that is the question;
     Whether 'tis nobler in the mind to suffer
     The slings and arrows of outrageous fortune,
     Or to take arms against a sea of troubles,
     And by opposing end them? To die, to sleep—
     No more; and by a sleep to say we end
     The heart-ache and the thousand natural
     shocks
     That flesh is heir to. 'Tis a consummation
     Devoutly to be wish'd. To die, to sleep;
     To sleep, perchance to dream. Ay, there's the
     rub;
     For in that sleep of death what dreams may
     come,
     When we have shuffled off this mortal coil,
     Must give us pause. There's the respect
     That makes calamity of so long life;
     For who would bear the whips and scorns of
     time,
     Th' oppressor's wrong, the proud man's
     contumely,

The pangs of despis'd love, the law's delay,
The insolence of office, and the spurns
That patient merit of th' unworthy takes,
When he himself might his quietus make
With a bare bodkin? Who would these fardels bear,
To grunt and sweat under a weary life,
But that the dread of something after death—
The undiscover'd country, from whose bourn
No traveller returns—puzzles the will,
And makes us rather bear those ills we have
Than fly to others that we know not of?
Thus conscience does make cowards of us all;
And thus the native hue of resolution
Is sicklied o'er with the pale cast of thought,
And enterprises of great pitch and moment,
With this regard, their currents turn awry
And lose the name of action.—Soft you now!
The fair Ophelia.—Nymph, in thy orisons
Be all my sins rememb'red.

OPH.	Good my lord,
	How does your honour for this many a day?
HAM.	I humbly thank you; well, well, well.
OPH.	My lord. I have remembrances of yours
	That I have longed long to re-deliver.
	I pray you now receive them.
HAM.	No, not I;
	I never gave you aught.

OPH.	My honour'd lord, you know right well you did,
	And with them words of so sweet breath compos'd
	As made the things more rich; their perfume lost,
	Take these again; for to the noble mind
	Rich gifts wax poor when givers prove unkind.
	There, my lord.
HAM.	Ha, ha! Are you honest?
OPH.	My lord?
HAM.	Are you fair?
OPH.	What means your lordship?
HAM.	That if you be honest and fair, your honesty should admit no discourse to your beauty.
OPH.	Could beauty, my lord, have better commerce than with honesty?
HAM.	Ay, truly; for the power of beauty will sooner transform honesty from what it is to a bawd than the force of honesty can translate beauty into his likeness. This was sometime a paradox, but now the time gives it proof. I did love you once.
OPH.	Indeed, my lord, you made me believe so.
HAM.	You should not have believ'd me; for virtue cannot so inoculate our old stock but we shall relish of it. I loved you not.

OPH.   I was the more deceived.

HAM.   Get thee to a nunnery. Why wouldst thou be
         a breeder of sinners? I am myself indifferent
         honest, but yet I could accuse me of such
         things that it were better my mother had not
         borne me: I am very proud, revengeful,
         ambitious; with more offences at my beck
         than I have thoughts to put them in,
         imagination to give them shape, or time to
         act them in. What should such fellows as I
         do crawling between earth and heaven? We
         are arrant knaves, all; believe none of us. Go
         thy ways to a nunnery. Where's your father?

OPH.   At home, my lord.

HAM.   Let the doors be shut upon him,
         that he may play the fool nowhere but in's
         own house. Farewell.

OPH.   O, help him, you sweet heavens!

HAM.   If thou dost marry, I'll give thee this plague
         for thy dowry: be thou as chaste as ice, as
         pure as snow, thou shalt not escape calumny.
         Get thee to a nunnery, go, farewell. Or, if
         thou wilt needs marry, marry a fool; for wise
         men know well enough what monsters you
         make of them. To a nunnery, go; and quickly
         too. Farewell.

OPH.   O heavenly powers, restore him!

HAM.   I have heard of your paintings too, well

enough; God hath given you one face, and you make yourselves another. You jig and amble, and you lisp, and nickname God's creatures, and make your wantonness your ignorance. Go to, I'll no more on't; it hath made me mad. I say we will have no moe marriage: those that are married already, all but one, shall live; the rest shall keep as they are. To a nunnery, go.   [*Exit.*

OPH. O, what a noble mind is here o'erthrown!
The courtier's, soldier's, scholar's, eye, tongue, sword;
Th' expectancy and rose of the fair state,
The glass of fashion and the mould of form,
Th' observ'd of all observers—quite, quite down!
And I, of ladies most deject and wretched,
That suck'd the honey of his music vows,
Now see that noble and most sovereign reason,
Like sweet bells jangled, out of time and harsh;
That unmatch'd form and feature of blown youth
Blasted with ecstasy. O, woe is me
T' have seen what I have seen, see what I see!

RE-ENTER KING AND POLONIUS.

KING. Love! His affections do not that way tend;

Nor what he spake, though it lack'd form a
little,
Was not like madness. There's something in
his soul
O'er which his melancholy sits on brood;
And I do doubt the hatch and the disclose
Will be some danger; which to prevent
I have in quick determination
Thus set it down: he shall with speed to
England
For the demand of our neglected tribute.
Haply the seas and countries different,
With variable objects, shall expel
This something-settled matter in his heart
Whereon his brains still beating puts him thus
From fashion of himself. What think you
on't?

POL.   It shall do well. But yet do I believe
The origin and commencement of his grief
Sprung from neglected love. How now,
Ophelia!
You need not tell us what Lord Hamlet said;
We heard it all. My lord do as you please;
But if you hold it fit, after the play
Let his queen mother all alone entreat him
To show his grief. Let her be round with him;
And I'll be plac'd, so please you, in the ear
Of all their conference. If she find him not,

To England send him; or confine him where
Your wisdom best shall think.

KING.   It shall be so;
Madness in great ones must not unwatch'd
go.   [*Exeunt.*

SCENE II

Elsinore. The Castle.

ENTER HAMLET AND THREE OF THE PLAYERS.

HAM.   Speak the speech, I pray you, as I pronounc'd
it to you, trippingly on the tongue; but if
you mouth it, as many of our players do, I
had as lief the town-crier spoke my lines. Nor
do not saw the air too much with your hand,
thus, but use all gently; for in the very torrent,
tempest, and, as I may say, whirlwind of your
passion, you must acquire and beget a
temperance that may give it smoothness. O,
it offends me to the soul to hear a robustious
periwig-pated fellow tear a passion to tatters,
to very rags, to split the ears of the
groundlings, who, for the most part, are
capable of nothing but inexplicable dumb
shows and noise. I would have such a fellow

	whipp'd for o'erdoing Termagant; it out-herods Herod. Pray you avoid it.

1 PLAY.   I warrant your honour.

HAM.   Be not too tame neither, but let your own discretion be your tutor. Suit the action to the word, the word to the action; with this special observance, that you o'erstep not the modesty of nature; for anything so o'erdone is from the purpose of playing, whose end, both at the first and now, was and is to hold, as 'twere, the mirror up to nature; to show virtue her own feature, scorn her own image, and the very age and body of the time his form and pressure. Now, this overdone or come tardy off, though it makes the unskilful laugh, cannot but make the judicious grieve; the censure of the which one must, in your allowance, o'erweigh a whole theatre of others. O, there be players that I have seen play—and heard others praise, and that highly—not to speak it profanely, that, neither having th' accent of Christians, not the gait of Christian, pagan, nor man, have so strutted and bellowed that I have thought some of Nature's journeymen had made men, and not made them well, they imitated humanity so abominably.

1 PLAY.   I hope we have reform'd that indifferently with us, sir.

HAM.   O, reform it altogether. And let those that
          play your clowns speak no more than is set
          down for them; for there be of them that
          will themselves laugh, to set on some
          quantity of barren spectators to laugh too,
          though in the meantime some necessary
          question of the play be then to be considered.
          That's villainous, and shows a most pitiful
          ambition in the fool that uses it. Go make
          you ready.   [*Exeunt Players.*

          ENTER POLONIUS, ROSENCRANTZ, AND
                    GUILDENSTERN.

          How now, my lord! Will the King hear this
          piece of work?

POL.   And the Queen too, and that presently.

HAM.   Bid the players make haste.   [*Exit Polonius.*
          Will you two help to hasten them?

ROS.   Ay, my lord.   [*Exeunt they two.*

HAM.   What, ho, Horatio!

                    ENTER HORATIO.

HOR.   Here, sweet lord, at your service.

HAM.   Horatio, thou art e'en as just a man
          As e'er my conversation cop'd withal.

HOR.   O my dear lord!

HAM.   Nay, do not think I flatter;
          For what advancement may I hope from
          thee,

That no revenue hast but thy good spirits
To feed and clothe thee? Why should the
poor be flatter'd?
No, let the candied tongue lick absurd
pomp,
And crook the pregnant hinges of the knee
Where thrift may follow fawning. Dost
thou hear?
Since my dear soul was mistress of her
choice
And could of men distinguish her election,
Sh'hath seal'd thee for herself; for thou hast
been
As one, in suff'ring all, that suffers nothing;
A man that Fortune's buffets and rewards
Hast ta'en with equal thanks; and blest are
those
Whose blood and judgment are so well
comeddled
That they are not a pipe for Fortune's finger
To sound what stop the please. Give me
that man
That is not passion's slave, and I will wear
him
In my heart's core, ay, in my heart of heart,
As I do thee. Something too much of this.
There is a play to-night before the King;
One scene of it comes near the circumstance
Which I have told thee of my father's death.

I prithee, when thou seest that act afoot,
Even with the very comment of thy soul
Observe my uncle. If his occulted guilt
Do not itself unkennel in one speech,
It is a damned ghost that we have seen,
And my imaginations are as foul
As Vulcan's stithy. Give him heedful note;
For I mine eyes will rivet to his face;
And, after, we will both our judgments join
In censure of his seeming.

HOR.   Well, my lord.
If 'a steal aught the whilst this play is playing.
And scape detecting, I will pay the theft.

ENTER TRUMPETS AND KETTLEDRUMS. DANISH
MARCH. SOUND A FLOURISH. ENTER KING, QUEEN,
POLONIUS, OPHELIA, ROSENCRANTZ, GUILDENSTERN,
AND OTHER LORDS ATTENDANT, WITH THE GUARD
CARRYING TORCHES.

HAM.   They are coming to the play; I must be idle.
Get you a place.

KING.   How fares our cousin Hamlet?

HAM.   Excellent, i' faith; of the chameleon's dish. I
eat the air, promise-cramm'd; you cannot feed
capons so.

KING.   I have nothing with this answers, Hamlet;
these words are not mine.

HAM.   No, nor mine now.   [*To Polonius*]
My lord, you play'd once i' th' university, you
say?

POL.   That did I, my lord, and was accounted a
         good actor.

HAM.   What did you enact?

POL.   I did enact Julius Cæsar; I was kill'd i' th'
         Capitol; Brutus kill'd me.

HAM.   It was a brute part of him to kill so capital a
         calf there. Be the players ready?

ROS.   Ay, my lord; they stay upon your patience.

QUEEN.   Come hither, my dear Hamlet, sit by me.

HAM.   No, good mother; here's metal more
         attractive.

POL.   [*To the King*] O, ho! do you mark that?

HAM.   Lady, shall I lie in your lap?
                              [*Lying down at Ophelia's feet.*

OPH.   No, my lord.

HAM.   I mean, my head upon your lap?

OPH.   Ay, my lord.

HAM.   Do you think I meant country matters?

OPH.   I think nothing, my lord.

HAM.   That's a fair thought to lie between maids'
         legs.

OPH.   What is, my lord?

HAM.   Nothing.

OPH.   You are merry, my lord.

HAM.   Who, I?

OPH.   Ay, my lord.

HAM.   O God, your only jig-maker! What should a
         man do but be merry? For look you how

cheerfully my mother looks, and my father died within's two hours.

OPH. Nay, 'tis twice two months, my lord.

HAM. So long? Nay then, let the devil wear black, for I'll have a suit of sables. O heavens! die two months ago, and not forgotten yet? Then there's hope a great man's memory may outlive his life half a year; but, by'r lady, 'a must build churches, then; or else shall 'a suffer not thinking on, with the hobby-horse, whose epitaph is 'For O, for O, the hobby-horse is forgot!'

The trumpet sounds. Hautboys play. The Dumb Show enters.

Enter a King and a Queen, very lovingly; the Queen embracing him and he her. She kneels, and makes show of protestation unto him. He takes her up, and declines his head upon her neck. He lies him down upon a bank of flowers; she, seeing him asleep, leaves him. Anon comes in a Fellow, takes off his crown, kisses it, pours poison in the sleeper's ears, and leaves him. The Queen returns; finds the King dead, and makes passionate action. The Poisoner, with some two or three Mutes, comes in again, seeming to condole with her. The dead body is carried away. The Poisoner woos the Queen with gifts:

	she seems harsh awhile, but in the end accepts his love. [*Exeunt.*
OPH.	What means this, my lord?
HAM.	Marry, this is miching mallecho; it means mischief.
OH.	Belike this show imports the argument of the play.

ENTER PROLOGUE.

HAM.	We shall know by this fellow: the players cannot keep counsel; they'll tell all.
OPH.	Will 'a tell us what this show meant?
HAM.	Ay, or any show that you will show him. Be not you asham'd to show, he'll not shame to tell you what it means.
OPH.	You are naught, you are naught. I'll mark the play.
PRO.	*For us, and our tragedy,* *Here stooping to your clemency,* *We beg your hearing patiently.* [*Exit.*
HAM.	Is this a prologue, or the posy of a ring?
OPH.	'Tis brief, my lord.
HAM.	As woman's love.

ENTER THE PLAYER KING AND QUEEN.

P. KING.	*Full thirty times hath Phœbus' cart gone round* *Neptune's salt wash and Tellus' orbed ground,* *And thirty dozen moons with borrowed sheen*

About the world have times twelve thirties
been,
Since love our hearts and Hymen did our hands
Unite comutual in most sacred bands.

P. QUEEN.   *So many journeys may the sun and moon*
Make us again count o'er ere love be done!
But, woe is me, you are so sick of late,
So far from cheer and from your former state,
That I distrust you. Yet, though I distrust,
Discomfort you, my lord, it nothing must;
For women fear too much even as they love,
And women's fear and love hold quantity,
In neither aught, or in extremity.
Now, what my love is, proof hath made you
know;
And as my love is siz'd, my fear is so.
Where love is great, the littlest doubts are fear;
Where little fears grow great, great love grows
there.

P. KING.   *Faith, I must leave thee, love, and shortly too:*
My operant powers their functions leave to do;
And thou shalt live in this fair world behind,
Honour'd, belov'd; and haply one as kind
For husband shalt thou—

P. QUEEN.   *O, confound the rest!*
Such love must needs be treason in my breast.
In second husband let me be accurst!
None wed the second but who kill'd the first.

HAM.   That's wormwood, wormwood.

P. QUEEN. *The instances that second marriage move*
Are base respects of thrift, but none of love.
A second time I kill my husband dead,
When second husband kisses me in bed.

P. KING. *I do believe you think what now you speak;*
But what we do determine oft we break.
Purpose is but the slave to memory,
Of violent birth, but poor validity;
Which now, the fruit unripe, sticks on the tree;
But fall unshaken when they mellow be.
Most necessary 'tis that we forget
To pay ourselves what to ourselves is debt.
What to ourselves in passion we propose,
The passion ending, doth the purpose lose.
The violence of either grief or joy
Their own enactures with themselves destroy.
Where joy most revels grief doth most lament;
Grief joys, joy grieves, on slender accident.
This world is not for aye; nor 'tis not strange
That even our loves should with our fortunes
change;
For 'tis a question left us yet to prove,
Whether love lead fortune or else fortune love.
The great man down, you mark his favourite
flies;
The poor advanc'd makes friends of enemies.
And hitherto doth love on fortune tend;
For who not needs shall never lack a friend,

And who in want a hollow friend both try,
Directly seasons him his enemy.
But, orderly to end where I begun,
Our wills and fates do so contrary run
That our devices still are overthrown;
Our thoughts are ours, their ends none of our
own.
So think thou will no second husband wed;
But die thy thoughts when thy first lord is dead.

P. QUEEN. *Nor earth to me give food, nor heaven light,*
Sport and repose lock from me day and night,
To desperation turn my trust and hope,
An anchor's cheer in prison be my scope,
Each opposite that blanks the face of joy
Meet what I would have well, and it destroy,
Both here and hence pursue me lasting strife,
If, once a widow, ever I be wife!

HAM.   If she should break it now!

P. KING. *'Tis deeply sworn. Sweet, leave me here awhile;*
My spirits grow dull, and fain I would beguile
The tedious day with sleep.   [Sleeps.

P. QUEEN. *Sleep rock thy brain,*
And never come mischance between us twain!
                                        [Exit.

HAM.   Madam, how like you this play?

QUEEN.   The lady doth protest too much, methinks.

HAM.   O, but she'll keep her word.

KING.   What do you call the play?

HAM.   'The Mouse-trap.' Marry, how? Tropically.
        This play is the image of a murder done in
        Vienna: Gonzago is the duke's name; his wife,
        Baptista. You shall see anon. 'Tis a knavish
        piece of work; but what of that? Your majesty,
        and we that have free souls, it touches us not.
        Let the galled jade wince, our withers are
        unwrung.

                    ENTER LUCIANUS.

        This is one Lucianus, nephew to the King.
OPH.   You are as good as a chorus, my lord.
HAM.   I could interpret between you and your love,
        if I could see the puppets dallying.
OPH.   You are keen, my lord, you are keen.
HAM.   It would cost you a groaning to take off mine
        edge.
OPH.   Still better, and worse.
HAM.   So you mis-take your husbands.—
        Begin, murderer; pox, leave thy damnable
        faces and begin. Come; the croaking raven
        doth bellow for revenge.
LUC.   *Thoughts black, hands apt, drugs fit, and time
        agreeing;*
        Confederate season, else no creature seeing;
        *Thou mixture rank, of midnight weeds
        collected,*
        With Hecat's ban thrice blasted, thrice infected,

> *Thy natural magic and dire property*
> *On wholesome life usurps immediately.*
> > [*Pours the poison in his ears.*

HAM. 'A poisons him i' th' garden for his estate. His name's Gonzago. The story is extant, and written in very choice Italian. You shall see anon how the murderer gets the love of Gonzago's wife.

OPH. The King rises.

HAM. What, frighted with false fire!

QUEEN. How fares my lord.

KING. Give me some light. Away!

POL. Lights, lights, lights!
> > [*Exeunt all but Hamlet and Horatio.*

HAM. Why, let the strucken deer go weep,
The hart ungalled play;
For some must watch, while some must sleep;
Thus runs the world away.
Would not this, sir, and a forest of feathers— if the rest of my fortunes turn Turk with me—with two Provincial roses on my raz'd shoes, get me a fellowship in a cry of players, sir?

HOR. Half a share.

HAM. A whole one, I.
For thou dost know, O Damon dear,
This realm dismantled was
Of Jove himself; and now reigns here

	A very, very—paiock.
HOR.	You might have rhym'd.
HAM.	O good Horatio, I'll take the ghost's word for a thousand pound. Didst perceive?
HOR.	Very well, my lord.
HAM.	Upon the talk of the poisoning.
HOR.	I did very well note him.
HAM.	Ah, ha! Come, some music. Come, the recorders.

> For if the King like not the comedy,
> Why, then, belike he likes it not, perdy.
> Come, some music.

RE-ENTER RESENCRANTZ AND GUILDENSTERN.

GUIL.	Good my lord, vouchsafe me a word with you.
HAM.	Sir, a whole history.
GUIL.	The King, sir—
HAM.	Ay, sir, what of him?
GUIL.	Is, in his retirement, marvellous distemp'red.
HAM.	With drink, sir?
GUIL.	No, my lord, rather with choler.
HAM.	Your wisdom should show itself more richer to signify this to his doctor; for for me to put him to his purgation would perhaps plunge him into far more choler.
GUIL.	Good my lord, put your discourse into some frame, and start not so wildly from my affair.

HAM.   I am tame, sir. Pronounce.

GUIL.   The Queen, your mother, in most great affliction of spirit, hath sent me to you.

HAM.   You are welcome.

GUIL.   Nay, good my lord, this courtesy is not of the right breed. If it shall please you to make me a wholesome answer, I will do your mother's commandment; if not, your pardon and my return shall be the end of my business.

HAM.   Sir, I cannot.

ROS.   What, my lord?

HAM.   Make you a wholesome answer; my wit's diseas'd. But, sir, such answer as I can make, you shall command; or rather, as you say, my mother. Therefore no more, but to the matter: my mother, you say—

ROS.   Then thus she says: your behaviour hath struck her into amazement and admiration.

HAM.   O wonderful son, that can so stonish a mother! But is there no sequel at the heels of this mother's admiration? Impart.

ROS.   She desires to speak with you in her closet ere you go to bed.

HAM.   We shall obey, were she ten times our mother. Have you any further trade with us?

ROS.   My lord, you once did love me.

HAM.   And do still, by these pickers and stealers.

ROS.   Good my lord, what is your cause of distemper? You do surely bar the door upon your own liberty, if you deny your griefs to

	your friend.
HAM.	Sir, I lack advancement.
ROS.	How can that be, when you have the voice of the King himself for your succession in Denmark?
HAM.	Ay, sir, but 'While the grass grows'—the proverb is something musty.

RE-ENTER THE PLAYERS, WITH RECORDERS.

	O, the recorders! Let me see one. To withdraw with you—why do you so about to recover the wind of me, as if you would drive me into a toil?
GUIL.	O my lord, if my duty be too bold, my love is too unmannerly.
HAM.	I do not well understand that. Will you play upon this pipe?
GUIL.	My lord, I cannot.
HAM.	I pray you.
GUIL.	Believe me, I cannot.
HAM.	I do beseech you.
GUIL.	I know no touch of it, my lord.
HAM.	It is as easy as lying: govern these ventages with your fingers and thumb, give it breath with your mouth, and it will discourse most eloquent music. Look you, these are the stops.
GUIL.	But these cannot I command to any utterance of harmony; I have not the skill.
HAM.	Why, look you now, how unworthy a thing you make of me! You would play upon me;

you would seem to know my stops; you would pluck out the heart of my mystery; you would sound me from my lowest note to the top of my compass; and there is much music, excellent voice, in this little organ, yet cannot you make it speak. 'Sblood, do you think I am easier to be play'd on than a pipe? Call me what instrument you will, though you can fret me, yet you cannot play upon me.

RE-ENTER POLONIUS.

God bless you, sir !

POL.   My lord, the Queen would speak with you, and presently.

HAM.   Do you see yonder cloud that's almost in shape of a camel?

POL.   By th' mass, and 'tis like a camel indeed.

HAM.   Methinks it is like a weasel.

POL.   It is back'd like a weasel.

HAM.   Or like a whale.

POL.   Very like a whale?

HAM.   Then I will come to my mother by and by [*Aside*] They fool me to the top of my bent.—I will come by and by.

POL.   I will say so.   [*Exit Polonius.*

HAM.   'By and by' is easily said. Leave me, friends.
                              [*Exeunt all but Hamlet.*
'Tis now the very witching time of night,

When churchyards yawn, and hell itself
breathes out
Contagion to this world. Now could I drink
hot blood,
And do such bitter business as the day
Would quake to look on. Soft! now to my
mother.
O heart, lose not thy nature; let not ever
The soul of Nero enter this firm bosom.
Let me be cruel, not unnatural:
I will speak daggers to her, but use none.
My tongue and soul in this be hypocrites—
How in my words somever she he shent,
To give them seals never, my soul, consent!
                                             [*Exit.*

SCENE III

Elsinore. The Castle.

ENTER KING, ROSENCRANTZ, AND GUILDENSTERN.

KING.   I like him not; not stands it safe with us
         To let his madness range. Therefore prepare
         you;
         I your commission will forthwith dispatch,
         And he to England shall along with you.
         The terms of our estate may not endure

	Hazard so near's as doth hourly grow
	Out of his brows.
GUIL.	We will ourselves provide.
	Most holy and religious fear it is
	To keep those many many bodies safe
	That live and feed upon your Majesty.
ROS.	The single and peculiar life is bound
	With all the strength and armour of the mind
	To keep itself from noyance; but much more
	That spirit upon whose weal depends and rests
	The lives of many. The case of majesty
	Dies not alone, but like a gulf both draw
	What's near it with it. It is a massy wheel,
	Fix'd on the summit of the highest mount,
	To whose huge spokes ten thousand lesser things
	Are mortis'd and adjoin'd; which when it falls,
	Each small annexment, petty consequence,
	Attends the boist'rous ruin. Never alone
	Did the king sigh, but with a general groan.
KING.	Arm you, I pray you, to this speedy voyage;
	For we will fetters put about this fear,
	Which now goes too free-footed.
ROS.	We will haste us.

        [*Exeunt Rosencrantz and Guildenstem.*

ENTER POLONIUS.

| POL. | My lord, he's going to his mother's closet. |

Behind the arras I'll convey myself
To hear the process. I'll warrant she'll tax him home;
And, as you said, and wisely was it said,
'Tis meet that some more audience than a mother,
Since nature makes them partial, should o'erhear
The speech, of vantage. Fare you well, my liege.
I'll call upon you ere you go to bed,
And tell you what I know.

KING.   Thanks, dear my lord.   [*Exit Polonius.*
O, my offence is rank, it smells to heaven;
It hath the primal eldest curse upon't—
A brother's murder! Pray can I not,
Though inclination be as sharp as will.
My stronger guilt defeats my strong intent,
And, like a man to double business bound,
I stand in pause where I shall first begin,
And both neglect. What if this cursed hand
Were thicker than itself with brother's blood,
Is there not rain enough in the sweet heavens
To wash it white as snow? Whereto serves mercy
But to confront the visage of offence?
And what's in prayer but this twofold force,
To be forestalled ere we come to fall,
Or pardon'd being down? Then I'll look up;

My fault is past. But, O, what form of prayer
Can serve my turn? 'Forgive me my foul
murder'!
That cannot be; since I am still possess'd
Of those effects for which I did the murder—
My crown, mine own ambition, and my
queen.
May one be pardon'd and retain th' offence?
In the corrupted currents of this world
Offence's gilded hand may shove by justice;
And oft 'tis seen the wicked prize itself
Buys out the law. But 'tis not so above:
There is no shuffling; there the action lies
In his true nature; and we ourselves compell'd,
Even to the teeth and forehead of our faults,
To give in evidence. What then? What rests?
Try what repentance can. What can it not?
Yet what can it when one can not repent?
O wretched state! O bosom black as death!
O limed soul, that, struggling to be free,
Art more engag'd! Help, angels. Make assay:
Bow, stubborn knees; and, heart, with strings
of steel,
Be soft as sinews of the new-born babe.
All may be well.   [*Retires and kneels.*

ENTER HAMLET.

HAM. Now might I do it pat, now 'a is a-praying;
And now I'll do't—and so 'a goes to heaven,

And so am I reveng'd. That would be scann'd:
A villian kills my father; and for that,
I, his sole son, do this same villain send
To heaven.
Why, this is hire and salary, not revenge.
'A took my father grossly, full of bread,
With all his crimes broad blown, as flush as
May;
And how his audit stands who knows save
heaven?
But in our circumstance and course of thought
'Tis heavy with him; and am I then reveng'd
To take him in the purging of his soul,
When he is fit and season'd for his passage?
No.
Up, sword, and know thou a more horrid
hent.
When he is drunk asleep, or in his rage;
Or in th' incestuous pleasure of his bed;
At game, a-swearing, or about some act
That has no relish of salvation in't—
Then trip him, that his heels may kick at
heaven,
And that his soul may be as damn'd and black
As hell, whereto it goes. My mother stays.
This physic but prolongs thy sickly days.
                                                    [*Exit.*

KING.   [*Rising*] My words fly up, my thoughts
         remain below.

Words without thought never to heaven go.
[*Exit.*

SCENE IV

The Queen's closet.

ENTER QUEEN AND POLONIUS.

POL.   'A will come straight. Look you lay home to
         him;
         Tell him his pranks have been too broad to
         bear with,
         And that your Grace hath screen'd and stood
         between
         Much heat and him. I'll silence me even here.
         Pray you be round with him.

HAM.   [*Within*] Mother, mother, mother!

QUEEN. I'll warrant you. Fear me not.
         Withdraw, I hear him coming.
                    [*Polonius goes behind the arras.*

ENTER HAMLET.

HAM.   Now, mother, what's the matter?

QUEEN. Hamlet, thou hast thy father much offended.

HAM.   Mother, you have my father much offended.

QUEEN. Come, come, you answer with an idle tongue.

HAM.   Go, go, you question with a wicked tongue.

QUEEN. Why, how now, Hamlet!

HAM.   What's the matter now?

QUEEN. Have you forgot me?

HAM.   No, by the rood, not so:
        You are the Queen, your husband's brother's
        wife;
        And—would it were not so!—you are my
        mother.

QUEEN. Nay then, I'll set those to you that can speak.

HAM.   Come, come, and sit you down; you shall
        not budge.
        You go not till I set you a glass
        Where you may see the inmost part of you.

QUEEN. What wilt thou do? Thou wilt not murder
        me?
        Help, help, ho!

POL.   [*Behind*] What, ho! help, help, help!

HAM.   [*Draws*] How now! a rat?
        Dead, for a ducat, dead!
        [*Kills Polonius with a pass through the arras.*

POL.   [*Behind*] O, I am slain!

QUEEN. O me, what hast thou done?

HAM.   Nay, I know not: Is it the King?

QUEEN. O, what a rash and bloody deed is this!

HAM.   A bloody deed!—almost as bad, good mother,
        As kill a King and marry with his brother.

QUEEN. As kill a king!

HAM.   Ay, lady, it was my word. [*Parting the arras.*
        · Thou wretched, rash, intruding fool, farewell!

I took thee for thy better. Take thy fortune;
Thou find'st to be too busy is some danger.
Leave wringing of your hands. Peace; sit you down,
And let me wring your heart; for so I shall,
If it be made of penetrable stuff;
If damned custom have not braz'd it so
That it be proof and bulwark against sense.

QUEEN.   What have I done that thou dar'st wag thy tongue
In noise so rude against me?

HAM.   Such an act
That blurs the grace and blush of modesty;
Calls virtue hypocrite; takes off the rose
From the fair forehead of an innocent love,
And sets a blister there; makes marriagevows
As false as dicers' oaths. O, such a deed
As from the body of contraction plucks
The very soul, and sweet religion makes
A rhapsody of words. Heaven's face does glow
O'er this solidity and compound mass
With heated visage, as against the doom—
Is thought-sick at the act.

QUEEN.   Ay me, what act,
That roars so loud and thunders in the index?

HAM.   Look here upon this picture and on this,
The counterfeit presentment of two brothers.
See what a grace was seated on this brow;
Hyperion's curls; the front of Jove himself;

An eye like Mars, to threaten and command;
A station like the herald Mercury
New lighted on a heaven-kissing hill—
A combination and a form indeed
Where every god did seem to set his seal,
To give the world assurance of a man.
This was your husband. Look you now what follows:
Here is your husband, like a mildew'd ear
Blasting his wholesome brother. Have you eyes?
Could you on this fair mountain leave to feed,
And batten on this moor? Ha! have you eyes?
You cannot call it love; for at your age
The heyday in the blood is tame, it's humble,
And waits upon the judgment; and what judgment
Would step from this to this? Sense, sure, you have,
Else could you not have motion; but sure that sense
Is apoplex'd; for madness would not err,
Nor sense to ecstasy was ne'er so thrall'd
But it reserv'd some quantity of choice
To serve in such a difference. What devil was't
That thus hath cozen'd you at hoodmanblind?
Eyes without feeling, feeling without sight,

Ears without hands or eyes, smelling sans all,
Or but a sickly part of one true sense
Could not so mope. O shame! where is thy
blush?
Rebellious hell,
If thou canst mutine in a matron's bones,
To flaming youth let virtue be as wax
And melt in her own fire; proclaim no shame
When the compulsive ardour gives the charge,
Since frost itself as actively doth burn,
And reason panders will.

QUEEN. O Hamlet, speak no more!
Thou turn'st my eyes into my very soul;
And there I see such black and grained spots
As will not leave their tinct.

HAM. Nay, but to live
In the rank sweat of an enseamed bed,
Stew'd in corruption, honeying and making
love
Over the nasty sty!

QUEEN. O, speak to me no more!
These words like daggers enter in my ears;
No more, sweet Hamlet.

HAM. A murderer and a villain!
A slave that is not twentieth part the tithe
Of your precedent lord; a vice of kings;
A cutpurse of the empire and the rule,
That from a shelf the precious diadem stole
And put it in his pocket!

QUEEN. No more!

ENTER GHOST.

HAM.   A king of shreds and patches—
         Save me, and hover o'er me with your wings,
         You heavenly guard! What would your
         gracious figure?

QUEEN. Alas, he's mad!

HAM.   Do you not come your tardy son to chide,
         Th' important acting of your dread command?
         O, say!

GHOST. Do not forget; this visitation
         Is but to whet thy almost blunted purpose.
         But look, amazement on thy mother sits.
         O, step between her and her fighting soul!
         Conceit in weakest bodies strongest works.
         Speak to her, Hamlet.

HAM.   How is it with you, lady?

QUEEN. Alas, how is't with you,
         That you do bend your eye on vacancy,
         And with th' incorporal air do hold discourse?
         Forth at your eyes your spirits wildly peep;
         And, as the sleeping soldiers in th' alarm,
         Your bedded hairs like life in excrements
         Start up and stand an end. O gentle son,
         Upon the heat and frame of thy distemper
         Sprinkle cool patience! Whereon do you
         look?

HAM.   On him, on him! Look you how pale he glares.
His form and cause conjoin'd, preaching to stones,
Would make them capable.—Do not look upon me,
Lest with this piteous action you convert
My stern effects; then what I have to do
Will want true colour—tears perchance for blood.

QUEEN. To whom do you speak this?

HAM.   Do you see nothing there?

QUEEN. No, nothing but ourselves.

HAM.   Why, look you there. Look how it steals away.
My father, in his habit as be liv'd !
Look where he goes even now out at the portal.   [*Exit Ghost.*

QUEEN. This is the very coinage of your brain.
This bodiless creation ecstasy
Is very cunning in.

HAM.   Ecstasy!
My pulse as yours doth temperately keep time,
And makes as healthful music. It is not madness
That I have utt'red. Bring me to the test,
And I the matter will re-word which madness
Would gambol from. Mother, for love of

grace,
Lay not that flattering unction to your soul,
That not your trespass but my madness speaks:
It will but skin and film the ulcerous place,
Whiles rank corruption, mining all within,
Infects unseen. Confess yourself to heaven;
Repent what's past; avoid what is to come;
And do not spread the compost on the weeds,
To make them ranker. Forgive me this my virtue;
For in the fatness of these pursy times
Virtue itself of vice must pardon beg,
Yea, curb and woo for leave to do him good.

QUEET.　O Hamlet, thou hast cleft my heart in twain.

HAM.　O, throw away the worser part of it,
And live the purer with the other half.
Good night—but go not to my uncle's bed;
Assume a virtue, if you have it not.
That monster custom, who all sense doth eat,
Of habits devil, is angel yet in this,
That to the use of actions fair and good
He likewise gives a frock or livery
That aptly is put on. Refrain to-night;
And that shall lend a kind of easiness
To the next abstinence; the next more easy;
For use almost can change the stamp of nature,
And either curb the devil, or throw him out,

With wondrous potency. Once more, good
night;
And when you are desirous to be blest,
I'll blessing beg of you. For this same lord
I do repent; but Heaven hath pleas'd it so,
To punish me with this, and this with me,
That I must be their scourge and minister.
I will bestow him, and will answer well
The death I gave him. So, again good night.
I must be cruel only to be kind;
Thus bad begins and worse remains behind.
One word more, good lady.

QUEEN. What shall I do?

HAM.   Not this, by no means, that I did you do;
Let the bloat King tempt you again to bed;
Pinch wanton on your cheek; call you his
mouse;
And let him, for a pair of reechy kisses,
Or paddling in your neck with his damn'd
fingers,
Make you to ravel all this matter out,
That I essentially am not in madness,
But mad in craft. 'Twere good you let him
know;
For who that's but a queen, fair, sober, wise,
Would from a paddock, from a bat, a gib,
Such dear concernings hide? Who would do
so?
No, in despite of sense and secrecy,

Unpeg the basket on the house's top,
Let the birds fly, and, like the famous ape,
To try conclusions, in the basket creep
And break your own neck down.

QUEEN. Be thou assur'd, if words be made of breath
And breath of life, I have no life to breathe
What thou hast said to me.

HAM. I must to England; you know that?

QUEEN. Alack, I had forgot. 'Tis so concluded on.

HAM. There's letters seal'd; and my two school-
fellows,
Whom I will trust as I will adders fang'd—
They bear the mandate; they must sweep my
way
And marshal me to knavery. Let it work;
For 'tis the sport to have the engineer
Hoist with his own petar; and't shall go hard
But I will delve one yard below their mines
And blow them at the moon. O, 'tis most
sweet
When in one line two crafts directly meet.
This man shall set me packing.
I'll lug the guts into the neighbour room.
Mother, good night. Indeed, this counsellor
Is now most still, most secret, and most grave,
Who was in life a foolish prating knave.
Come, sir, to draw toward an end with you.
Good night, mother.
[*Exeunt severally; Hamlet tugging in Polonius.*

ACT IV SCENE I

Elsinore. The Castle.

ENTER KING, QUEEN, ROSENCRANTZ, AND
GUILDENSTERN.

KING.   There's matter in these sighs, these profound
heaves,
You must translate; 'tis fit we understand
them.
Where is your son?

QUEEN. Bestow this place on us a little while.
        [*Exeunt Rosencrantz and Guildenstern.*
Ah, mine own lord, what have I seen to-night!

KING.   What, Gertrude? How does Hamlet?

QUEEN. Mad as the sea and wind, when both contend
Whichis the mightier. In his lawless fit,

         Behind the arras hearing something
         Whips out his rapier, cries 'A rat! A rat!'
         And in this brainish apprehension kills
         The unseen good old man.

KING.   O heavy deed!
         It had been so with us had we been there.
         His liberty is full of threats to all—
         To you yourself, to us, to every one.
         Alas, how shall this bloody deed be answer'd?
         It will be laid to us, whose providence
         Should have kept short, restrain'd, and out of haunt,
         This mad young man. But so much was our love,
         We would not understand what was most fit;
         But, like the owner of a foul disease,
         To keep it from divulging, let it feed
         Even on the pith of life. Where is he gone?

QUEEN. To draw apart the body he hath kill'd;
         O'er whom his very madness, like some ore
         Among a mineral of metals base,
         Show itself pure: 'a weeps for what is done.

KING.   O Gertrude, come away!
         The sun no sooner shall the mountains touch
         But we will ship him hence; and this vile deed
         We must with all our majesty and skill
         Both countenance and excuse. Ho, Guildenstern!

RE-ENTER ROSENCRANTZ AND GUILDENSTERN.

Friends, both go join you with some further
aid;
Hamlet in madness hath Polonius slain,
And from his mother's closet hath he dragg'd
him;
Go seek him out; speak fair, and bring the
body
Into the chapel. I pray you haste in this.
            [*Exeunt Rosencrantz and Guildenstern.*
Come, Gertrude, we'll call up our wisest
friends
And let them know both what we mean to
do
And what's untimely done; so haply slander—
Whose whisper o'er the world's diameter,
As level as the cannon to his blank,
Transports his pois'ned shot—may miss our
name,
And hit the woundless air. O, come away!
My soul is full of discord and dismay.
                                    [*Exeunt.*

SCENE II

Elsinore. The Castle.

ENTER HAMLET.

HAM.   'Safely stow'd.
GENTLEMEN. [*Within*] Hamlet! Lord Hamlet!
HAM.   But soft! What noise? Who calls on Hamlet?
            O, here they come!

ENTER ROSENCRANTZ AND GUILDENSTERN.

ROS.   What have you done, my lord, with the dead
            body?
HAM.   Compounded it with dust, whereto 'tis kin.
ROS.   Tell us where 'tis, that we may take it thence
            And bear it to the chapel.
HAM.   Do not believe it.
ROS.   Believe what?
HAM.   That I can keep your counsel, and not mine
            own. Besides, to be demanded of a sponge—
            what replication should be made by the son
            of a king?
ROS.   Take you me for a sponge, my lord?
HAM.   Ay, sir; that soaks up the King's countenance,
            his rewards, his authorities. But such officers
            do the King best service in the end: he keeps
            them, like an ape an apple in the corner of his
            jaw; first mouth'd, to be last swallowed; when

	he needs what you have glean'd, it is but squeezing you and, sponge, you shall be dry again.
ROS.	I understand you not, my lord.
HAM.	I am glad of it; a knavish speech sleeps in a foolish ear.
ROS.	My lord, you must tell us where the body is, and go with us to the King.
HAM.	The body is with the King, but the King is not with the body. The King is a thing—
GUIL.	A thing, my lord!
HAM.	Of nothing. Bring me to him.
	Hide fox, and all after. [*Exeunt.*

SCENE III

Elsinore. The Castle.

Enter King, attended.

KING.	I have sent to seek him, and to find the body.

How dangerous is it that this man goes loose!
Yet must not we put the strong law on him:
He's lov'd of the distracted multitude,
Who like not in their judgment but their eyes;
And where 'tis so, th' offender's scourge is weigh'd,
But never the offence. To bear all smooth and even,

This sudden sending him away must seem
Deliberate pause. Diseases desperate grown
By desperate appliance are reliev'd,
Or not at all.

ENTER ROSENCRANTZ.

How now! what hath befall'n?

ROS.   Where the dead body is bestow'd, my lord,
          We cannot get from him.

KING.   But where is he?

ROS.   Without, my lord; guarded, to know your
          pleasure.

KING.   Bring him before us.

ROS.   Ho, Guildenstern! bring in the lord.

ENER HAMLET AND GUILDENSTERN.

KING.   Now, Hamlet, where's Polonius?

HAM.   At supper.

KING.   At supper! Where?

HAM.   Not where he eats, but where 'a is eaten; a
          certain convocation of politic worms are e'en
          at him. Your worm is your only emperor for
          diet: we fat all creatures else to fat us, and we
          fat ourselves for maggots; your fat king and
          your lean beggar is but variable service—two
          dishes, but to one table. That's the end.

KING.   Alas, alas!

HAM.   A man may fish with the worm that hath eat

of a king, and eat of the fish that hath fed of
that worm.

KING. What dost thou mean by this?

HAM. Nothing but to show you how a king may
go a progress through the guts of a begger.

KING. Where is Polonius?

HAM. In heaven; send thither to see; if your
messenger find him not there, seek him i' th'
other place yourself. But if, indeed, you find
him not within this month, you shall nose
him as you go up the stairs into the lobby.

KING. [*To Attendants*] Go seek him there.

HAM. 'A will stay till you come.

[*Exeunt Attendants.*

KING. Hamlet, this deed, for thine especial safety—
Which we do tender, as we dearly grieve
For that which thou hast done—must send
thee hence
With fiery quickness. Therefore prepare
thyself;
The bark is ready, and the wind at help,
Th' associates tend, and everything is bent
For England.

HAM. For England!

KING. Ay, Hamlet.

HAM. Good!

KING. So is it, if thou knew'st our purposes.

HAM. I seen a cherub that sees them.
But, come; for England! Farewell, dear

mother.

KING.   Thy loving father, Hamlet.

HAM.   My mother: father and mother is man and
          wife; man and wife is one flesh; and so, my
          mother. Come, for England.   [*Exit.*

KING.   Follow him at foot; tempt him with speed
          aboard;
          Delay it not; I'll have him hence to-night.
          Away! for everything is seal'd and done
          That else leans on th' affair. Pray you make
          haste.   [*Exeunt all but the King.*
          And, England, if my love thou hold'st at
          aught—
          As my great power thereof may give thee
          sense,
          Since yet thy cicatrice looks raw and red
          After the Danish sword, and thy free awe
          Pays homage to us—thou mayst not coldly
          set
          Our sovereign process; which imports at full,
          By letters conguring to that effect,
          The present death of Hamlet. Do it, England:
          For like the hectic in my blood he rages.
          And thou must cure me. Till I know 'tis done,
          Howe'er my haps, my joys were ne'er begun.
                              [*Exit.*

SCENE IV

A plain in Denmark.

ENTER FORTINBRAS WITH HIS ARMY OVER THE STAGE.

FORT.   Go, Captain, from me greet the Danish king.
        Tell him that by his licence Fortinbras
        Craves the conveyance of a promis'd march
        Over his kingdom. You know the rendezvous.
        If that his Majesty would aught with us,
        We shall express our duty in his eye;
        And let him know so.

CAP.   I will do't, my lord.

FORT.   Go softly on.   [*Exeunt all but the Captain.*

        ENTER HAMLET, ROSENCRANTZ,
          GUILDENSTERN, AND OTHERS.

HAM.   Good sir, whose powers are these?

CAP.   They are of Norway, sir.

HAM.   How purpos'd, sir, I pray you?

CAP.   Against some part of Poland.

HAM.   Who commands them, sir?

CAP.   The nephew to old Norway, Fortinbras.

HAM.   Goes it against the main of Poland, sir,
        Or for some frontier?

CAP.   Truly to speak, and with no addition,
        We go to gain a little patch of ground
        That hath in it no profit but the name.

	To pay five ducats, five, I would not farm it;

To pay five ducats, five, I would not farm it;
Nor will it yield to Norway or the Pole
A ranker rate should it be sold in fee.

HAM. Why, then the Polack never will defend it.

CAP. Yes, it is already garrison'd.

HAM. Two thousand soul and twenty thousand ducats
Will not debate he question of this straw.
This is th' imposthume of much wealth and peace,
That inward breaks, and shows no cause without
Why the man dies. I humbly thank you sir.

CAP. God buy you, sir.   [*Exit.*

ROS. Will't please you go, my lord?

HAM. I'll be with you straight. Go a litte before.
                    [*Exeunt all but Hamlet.*

How all occasions do inform against me,
And spur my dull revenge! What is a man,
If his chief good and market of his time
Be but to sleep and feed? A beast, no more!
Sure he that made us with such large discourse,
Looking before and after, gave us not
That capability and godlike reason
To fust in us unus'd. Now, whether it be
Bestial oblivion, or some craven scruple
Of thinking too precisely on th' event—

A thought which, quarter'd, hath but one part
wisdom
And ever three parts coward—I do not know
Why yet I live to say 'This thing's to do',
Sith I have cause, and will, and strength, and
means,
To do't. Examples gross as earth exhort me:
Witness this army, of such mass and charge,
Led by a delicate and tender prince,
Whose spirit, with divine ambition puff'd,
Makes mouths at the invisible event,
Exposing what is mortal and unsure
To all that fortune, death, and danger, dare,
Even for an egg-shell. Rightly to be great
Is not to stir without great argument,
But greatly to find quarrel in a straw,
When honour's at the stake. How stand I,
then,
That have a father kill'd, a mother stain'd,
Excitements of my reason and my blood,
And let all sleep, while to my shame I see
The imminent death of twenty thousand men
That, for a fantasy and trick of fame,
Go to their graves like beds, fight for a plot
Whereon the numbers cannot try the cause,
Which is not tomb enough and continent
To hide the slain? O, from this time forth,
My thoughts be bloody, or be nothing worth!
                                    [*Exit.*

SCENE V

Elsinore. The Castle.

ENTER QUEEN, HORATIO, AND A GENTLEMAN.

QUEEN. I will not speak with her.
GENT.   She is importunate, indeed distract.
              Her mood will needs be pitied.
QUEEN. What would see have?
GENT.   She speaks much of her father; says she hears
              There's tricks i' th' world, and hems, and beats
              her heart;
              Spurns enviously at straws; speaks things in
              doubt,
              That carry but half sense. Her speech is
              nothing,
              Yet the unshaped use of it doth move
              The hearers to collection; they yawn at it,
              And botch the words up fit to their own
              thoughts;
              Which, as her winks and nods and gestures
              yield them,
              Indeed would make one think there might
              be thought,
              Though nothing sure, yet much unhappily.
HOR.   'Twere good she were spoken with; for she
              may strew
              Dangerous conjectures in ill-breeding minds.

QUEEN. Let her come in   [*Exit Gentleman.*
        [*Aside*] To my sick soul, as sin's true nature is,
        Each toy seems prologue to some great amiss.
        So full of artless jealousy is guilt,
        It spills itself in fearing to be spilt.

        ENTER OPHELIA DISTRACTED.

OPH.   Where is the beautous Majesty of Denmark?
QUEEN. How now, Ophelia!
OPH.   [*Signs*]
        How should I your true love know
        From another one?
        By his cockle hat and staff,
        And his sandal shoon.
QUEEN. Alas, sweet lady, what imports this song?
OPH.   Say you? Nay, pray you mark.
        [*Sings*] He is dead and gone, lady,
        He is dead and gone;
        At his head a grass-green turf,
        At his heels a stone.
        O, ho !
QUEEN. Nay, but, Ophelia—
OPH.   Pray you mark.
        [*Sings*] White his shroud as the mountain
        snow—

        ENTER KING.

QUEEN. Alas, look here, my lord.

OPH.   Larded with sweet flowers;
          Which bewept to the grave did not go
          With true-love showers.

KING.   How do you, pretty lady?

OPH.   Well, God dild you! They say the owl was a
          baker's daughter. Lord, we know what we are,
          but know not what we may be. God be at
          your table!

KING.   Conceit upon her father.

OPH.   Pray let's have no words of this; but when
          they ask you what it means, say you this:
          [*Sings*] To-morrow is Saint Valentine's day,
          All in the morning betime,
          And I a maid at your window,
          To be your Valentine.

          Then up he rose, and donn'd his clothes,
          And dupp'd the chamber-door;
          Let in the maid, that out a maid
          Never departed more.

KING.   Pretty Ophelia!

OPH.   Indeed, la, without an oath, I'll make an end
          on't.
          [*Sings*] By Gis and by Saint Charity,
          Alack, and fie for shame!
          Young men will do't, if they come to't;
          By Cock, they are to blame.
          Quoth she 'Before you tumbled me,
          You promis'd me to wed'.

He answers:

'So would I 'a done, by yonder sun,

An thou hadst not come to my bed.'

KING. How long hath she been thus?

OPH. I hope all will be well. We must be patient;
but I cannot choose but weep to think they
would lay him i' th' cold ground. My brother
shall know of it; and so I thank you for your
good counsel. Come, my coach! Good night,
ladies; good night, sweet ladies, good night,
good night.   [*Exit.*

KING. Follow her close; give her good watch, I pray
you.   [*Exeunt Horatio and Gentleman.*
O, this is the poison of deep grief; it springs
All from her father's death. And now
behold—
O Gertrude, Gertrude!
When sorrows come, they come not single
spies,
But in battalions! First, her father slain;
Next, your son gone, and he most violent
author
Of his own just remove; the people muddied,
Thick and unwholesome in their thoughts
and whipers
For good Polonius' death; and we have done
but greenly
In hugger-mugger to inter him; poor Ophelia

Divided from herself and her fair judgment,
Without the which we are pictures, or mere
beasts;
Last, and as much containing as all these,
Her brother is in secret come from France;
Feeds on his wonder, keeps himself in clouds,
And wants not buzzers to infect his ear
With pestilent speeches of his father's death;
Wherein necessity, of matter beggar'd,
Will nothing stick our person to arraign
In ear and ear. O my dear Gertrude, this,
Like to a murd'ring piece, in many places
Gives me superfluous death. [*A noise within.*

QUEEN. Alack, what noise is this?
KING.   Attend!

ENTER A GENTLEMAN.

Where are my Switzers? Let them guard the
door.
What is the matter?
GENT.   Save yourself, my lord:
The ocean, overpeering of his list,
Eats not the flats with more impitious haste
Than young Laertes, in a riotous head,
O'erbears your officers. The rabble call him
lord;
And, as the world were now but to begin,
Antiquity forgot, custom not known,

The ratifiers and props of every word,
They cry 'Choose we; Laertes shall be king'.
Caps, hands, and tongues, applaud it to the
clouds,
'Laertes shall be king, Laertes king.'

QUEEN. How cheerfully on the false trail they cry!
                                        [*Noise within.*

O, this is counter, you false Danish dogs!

KING. The doors are broke.

ENTER LAERTES, WITH OTHERS, IN ARMS.

LAER. Where is this king ?—Sirs, stand you all
without.

ALL. No, let's come in.

LAER. I pray you give me leave.

ALL. We will, we will.   [*Exeunt.*

LAER. I thank you. Keep the door.—O thou vile
king,
Give me my father!

QUEEN. Calmly, good Laertes.

LAER. That drop of blood that's calm proclaims
me bastard;
Cries cuckold to my father; brands the
harlot
Even here, between the chaste unsmirched
brow
Of my true mother.

KING. What is the cause, Laertes,

That thy rebellion looks so giant-like?
Let him go, Gertrude; do not fear our person:
There's such divinity doth hedge a king
That treason can but peep to what it would,
Acts little of his will. Tell me, Laertes,
Why thou art thus incens'd. Let him go,
Gertrude.
Speak, man.

LEAR.   Where is my father?
KING.   Dead.
QUEEN.   But not by him.
KING.   Let him demand his fill.
LAER.   How came he dead? I'll not be juggled with.
To hell, allegiance! Vows, to the blackest devil!
Conscience and grace, to the profoundest pit!
I dare damnation. To this point I stand,
That both the worlds I give to negligence,
Let come what comes; only I'll be reveng'd
Most throughly for my father.
KING.   Who shall stay you?
LAER.   My will, not all the world's.
And for my means, I'll husband them so well
They shall go far with little.
KING.   Good Laertes,
If you desire to know the certainty
Of your dear father, is't writ in your revenge
That, swoopstake, you will draw both friend
and foe,

	Winner and loser?
LAER.	None but his enemies.
KING.	Will you know them, then?
LEAR.	To his good friends thus wide I'll ope my arms And, like the kind life-rend'ring pelican, Repast them with my blood.
KING.	Why, now you speak Like a good child and a true gentleman. That I am guiltless of your father's death, And am most sensibly in grief for it, It shall as level to your judgment 'pear As day does to your eye.

          [*A noise within:* 'Let her come in.'

LEAR.	How now! What noise is that.

RE-ENTER OPHELLA.

O, heat dry up my brains! tears seven times salt
Burn out the sense and virtue of mine eye!
By heaven, thy madness shall be paid with weight
Till our scale turn the beam. O rose of May!
Dear maid, kind sister, sweet Ophelia!
O heavens! is't possible a young maid's wits
Should be as mortal as an old man's life?
Nature is fine in love; and where 'tis fine
It sends some precious instance of itself

After the thing it loves.

OPH.   [*Sings*] They bore him barefac'd on the bier;
Hey non nonny, nonny, hey nonny;
And in his grave rain'd many a tear—

Fare you well, my dove!

LAER.   Hadst thou thy wits, and didst persuade revenge,
It could not move thus.

OPH.   You must sing 'A-down, a-down', an you call
him a-down-a. O, how the wheel becomes
it! It is the false steward, that stole his master's
daughter.

LAER.   This nothing's more than matter.

OPH.   There's rosemary, that's for remembrance;
pray you, love, remember. And there is
pansies, that's for thoughts.

LAER.   A document in madness—thoughts and
remembrance fitted.

OPH.   There's fennel for you, and columbines.
There's rue for you; and here's some for me.
We may call it herb of grace a Sundays. O,
you must wear your rue with a difference.
There's a daisy. I would give you some violets,
but they wither'd all when my father died.
They say 'a made a good end.
[*Sings*] For bonny sweet Robin is all my joy.

LAER.   Thought and affliction, passion, hell itself,
She turns to favour and to prettiness.

OPH.   [*Sings*] And will 'a not come again?
            And will 'a not come again?
            No, no, he is dead,
            Go to thy death-bed,
            He never will come again.

            His beard was as white as snow,
            All flaxen was his poll;
            He is gone, he is gone,
            And we cast away moan:
            God-a-mercy on his soul!
            And of all Christian souls, I pray God. God
            buy you.   [*Exit.*

LAER.   Do you see this, O God?

KING.   Leartes, I must commune with your grief.
            Or you deny me right. Go but apart,
            Make choice of whom your wisest friends
            you will,
            And they shall hear and judge 'twixt you and
            me.
            If by direct or by collateral hand
            They find us touch'd, we will our kingdom
            give,
            Our crown, our life, and all that we call ours,
            To you in satisfaction; but if not,
            Be you content to lend your patience to us,
            And we shall jointly labour with your soul
            To give it due content.

LEAR.   Let this be so.

His means of death, his obscure funeral—
No trophy, sword, nor hatchment, o'er his
bones,
No noble rite nor formal ostentation—
Cry to be heard, as 'twere from heaven to
earth,
That I must call't in question.

KING.   So you shall;
And where th' offence is, let the great axe fall.
I pray you go with me.   [*Exeunt.*

SCENE VI

Elsinore. The Castle.

ENTER HORATIO WITH AN ATTENDANT.

HOR.   What are they that would speak with me?
ATT.   Sea-faring men, sir; they say they have letters
for you.
HOR.   Let them come in.   [*Exit Attendant.*
I do not know from what part of the world
I should be greeted, if not from Lord Hamlet.

ENTER SAILORS.

SAIL.   God bless you, sir.
HOR.   Let Him bless thee too.
SAIL.   'A shall, sir, an't please Him.
There's a letter for you, sir; it came from th'

ambassador that was bound for England—if your name be Horatio, as I am let to know it is.

HOR.   [*Reads*] 'Horatio, when thou shalt have overlook'd this, give these fellows some means to the King: they have letters for him. Ere we were two days old at sea, a pirate of very warlike appointment gave us chase. Finding ourselves too slow of sail, we put on a compelled valour; and in the grapple I boarded them. On the instant they got clear of our ship; so I alone became their prisoner. They have dealt with me like thieves of mercy; but they knew what they did: I am to do a good turn for them. Let the King have the letters I have sent; and repair thou to me with as much speed as thou wouldest fly death. I have words to speak in thine ear will make thee dumb; yet are they much too light for the bore of the matter. These good fellows will bring thee where I am. Rosencrantz and Guildenstern hold their course for England; of them I have much to tell thee. Farewell.
He that thou knowest thine, HAMLET.'
Come, I will give you way for these your letters,
And do't the speedier that you may direct me
To him from whom you brought them.

[*Exeunt.*

SCENE VII

Elsinore. The Castle.

ENTER KING AND LAERTES.

KING.   Now must your conscience my acquittance
seal,
And you must put me in your heart for
friend,
Sith you have heard, and with a knowing ear,
That he which hath your noble father slain
Pursu'd my life.

LAER.   It well appears. But tell me
Why you proceeded not against these feats,
So crimeful and so capital in nature,
As by your safety, wisdom, all things else,
You mainly were stirr'd up.

KING.   O, for two special reasons,
Which may to you, perhaps, seem much
unsinew'd,
But yet to me th'are strong. The Queen his
mother
Lives almost by his looks; and for myself,
My virtue or my plague, be it either which—
She is so conjunctive to my life and soul
That, as the star moves not but in his sphere,
I could not but by her. The other motive,
Why to a public count I might not go,

Is the great love the general gender bear him;
Who, dipping all his faults in their affection,
Work like the spring that turneth wood to
stone,
Convert his gyves to graces; so that my
arrows,
Too slightly timber'd for so loud a wind,
Would have reverted to my bow again,
But not where I have aim'd them.

LAER.   And so have I a noble father lost;
A sister driven into desp'rate terms,
Whose worth, if praises may go back again,
Stood challenger on mount of all the age
For her perfections. But my revenge will
come.

KING.   Break not your sleeps for that. You must not
think
That we are made of stuff so flat and dull
That we can let our beard be shook with
danger,
And think it pastime. You shortly shall hear
more.
I lov'd your father, and we love our self;
And that, I hope, will teach you to imagine—

ENTER A MESSENGER WITH LETTERS.

How now! What news?

MESS.   Letters, my lord, from Hamlet:

	These to your Majesty; this to the Queen.
KING.	From Hamlet! Who brought them?
MESS.	Sailors, my lord, they say; I saw them not.
	They were given me by Claudio; he receiv'd them
	Oh him that brought them.
KING.	Laertes, you shall hear them.
	Leave us. [*Exit Messenger.*
	[*Reads*] 'High and Mighty. You shall know I am set naked on your kingdom. Tomorrow shall I beg leave to see your kingly eyes; when I shall, first asking your pardon thereunto, recount the occasion of my sudden and more strange return. HAMLET.'
	What should this mean? Are all the rest come back?
	Or is it some abuse, and no such thing?
LAER.	Know you the hand?
KING.	'Tis Hamlet's character. 'Naked'!
	And in a postcript here, he says 'alone'.
	Can you devise me?
LAER.	I am lost in it, my lord. But let him come;
	It warms the very sickness in my heart
	That I shall live and tell him to his teeth
	'Thus didest thou'.
KING.	If it be so, Laertes—
	As how should it be so, how otherwise?—
	Will you be rul'd by me?

LAER.   Ay, my lord;
         So you will not o'errule me to a peace.
KING.   To thine own peace. If he be now return'd.
         As checking at his voyage, and that he means
         No more to undertake it, I will work him
         To an exploit now ripe in my device,
         Under the which he shall not choose but fall;
         And for his death, no wind of blame shall
         breathe;
         But even his mother shall uncharge the
         practice
         And call it accident.
LAER.   My lord, I will be rul'd
         The rather, if you could devise it so
         That I might be the organ.
KING.   It falls right.
         You have been talk'd of since your travel much,
         And that in Hamlet's hearing, for a quality
         Wherein they say you shine. Your sum of
         parts
         Did not together pluck such envy from him
         As did that one; and that, in my regard,
         Of the unworthiest siege.
LAER.   What part is that, my lord?
KING.   A very riband in the cap of youth,
         Yet needful too; for youth no less becomes
         The light and careless livery that it wears
         Than settled age his sables and his weeds,

Importing health and graveness. Two months since
Here was a gentleman of Normandy—
I have seen myself, and serv'd against, the French,
And they can well on horseback; but this gallant
Had witchcraft in't; he grew unto his seat,
And to such wondrous doing brought his horse,
As had he been incorps'd an demi-natur'd
With the brave beast. So far he topp'd my thought,
That I, in forgery of shapes and tricks,
Come short of what he did.

LAER.   A Norman was't?
KING.   A Norman.
LAER.   Upon my life, Lamond.
KING.   The very same.
LAER.   I know him well. He is the brooch indeed
And gem of all the nation.
KING.   He made confession of you;
And gave you such a masterly report
For art and exercise in your defence,
And for your rapier most especial,
That he cried out 'twould be a sight indeed
If one could match you. The scrimers of their nation

He swore had neither motion, guard, nor eye,
If you oppos'd them. Sir, this report of his
Did Hamlet so envenom with his envy
That he could nothing do but wish and beg
Your sudden coming o'er, to play with you.
Now, out of this—

LAER. What out of this, my lord?

KING. Laertes, was your father dear to you?
Or are you like the painting of a sorrow,
A face without a heart?

LAER. Why ask you this?

KING. Not that I think you did not love your father;
But that I know love is begun by time,
And that I see, in passages of proof,
Time qualifies the spark and fire of it.
There lives within the very flame of love
A kind of wick or snuff that will abate it;
And nothing is at a like goodness still;
For foodness, growing to a pleurisy,
Dies in his own too much. That we would do,
We should do when we would; for this 'would' changes,
And hath abatements and delays as many
As there are tongues, are hands, are accidents;
And then this 'should' is like a spendthirft's sigh
That hurts by easing. But to the quick of th' ulcer:

Hamlet comes back; what would you undertake

To show yourself in deed your father's son More than in words?

LAER.   To cut his throat i' th' church.

KING.   No place, indeed, should murder sanctuarize; Revenge should have no bounds. But, good Laertes,

Will you do this? Keep close within your chamber.

Hamlet return'd shall know you are come home.

We'll put on those shall praise your excellence, And set a double varnish on the fame

The Frenchman gave you; bring you, in fine, together,

And wager on your heads. He, being remiss, Most generous, and free from all contriving, Will not peruse the foils; so that with ease Or with a little shuffling, you may choose. A sword unbated, and, in a pass of practice, Requite him for your father.

LAER.   I will do't;

And for that purpose I'll anoint my sword. I bought an unction of a mountebank, So mortal that but dip a knife in it, Where it draws blood no cataplasm so rare, Collected from all simples that have virtue

Under the moon, can save the thing from
death

That is but scratch'd withal. I'll touch my
point

With this contagion, that, if I gall him slightly,

It may be death.

KING.   Let's further think of this;

Weigh what convenience both of time and
means

May fit us to our shape. If this should fail,

And that our drift look through our bad
performance,

'Twere better not assay'd, therefore this project

Should have a back or second, that might hold

If this did blast in proof. Soft! let me see.

We'll make a solemn wager on your
cunnings—

I ha't.

When in your motion you are hot and dry—

As make your bouts more violent to that
end—

And that he calls for drink, I'll have preferr'd
him

A chalice for the nonce; whereon but sipping,

If he by chance escape your venom'd stuck,

Our purpose may hold there. But stay; what
noise?

ENTER QUEEN.

QUEEN. One woe doth tread upon another's heel,
So fast they follow. Your sister's drown'd,
Laertes.

LAER. Drown'd! O, where?

QUEEN. There is a willow grows aslant the brook
That shows his hoar leaves in the glassy stream;
Therewith fantastic garlands did she make
Of crowflowers, nettles, daisies, and long
purples
That liberal shepherds give a grosser name,
But our cold maids do dead men's fingers call
them.
There, on the pendent boughs her coronet
weeds
Clamb'ring to hang, an envious sliver broke;
When down her weedy trophies and herself
Fell in the weeping brook. Her clothes spread
wide
And, mermaid-like, awhile they bore her up;
Which time she chanted snatches of old lauds,
As one incapable of her own distress,
Or like a creature native and indued
Unto that element; but long it could not be
Till that her garments, heavy with their drink,
Pull'd the poor wretch from her melodious
lay
To muddy death.

LAER.   Alas, then she is drown'd!
QUEEN.   Drown'd, drown'd.
LAER.   Too much of water hast thou, poor Ophelia,
          And therefore I forbid my tears; but yet
          It is our trick; nature her custom holds,
          Let shame say what it will. When these are
          gone,
          The woman will be out. Adieu, my lord.
          I have a speech o' fire that fain would blaze
          But that this folly douts it.   [*Exit.*
KING.   Let's follow, Gertrude.
          How much I had to do to calm his rage!
          Now fear I this will give it start again;
          Therefore let's follow.   [*Exeunt.*

ACT V SCENE I
Elsinore. A churchyard.

ENTER TWO CLOWNS WITH SPADES AND PICKS.

1 CLO.   Is she to be buried in Christian burial when she wilfully seeks her own salvation?

2 CLO.   I tell thee she is; therefore make her grave straight. The crowner hath sat on her, and finds it Christian burial.

1 CLO.   How can that be, unless she drown'd herself in her own defence?

2 CLO.   Why, 'tis found so.

1 CLO.   It must be 'se offendendo'; it cannot be else. For here lies the point: if I drown myself wittingly, it argues an act; and an act hath three branches—it is to act, to do, to perform;

	argal, she drown'd herself wittingly.
2 CLO.	Nay, but hear you, Goodman Delver.
1 CLO.	Give me leave. Here lies the water; good. Here stands the man; good. If the man go to this water and drown himself, it is, will he, nill he, he goes—mark you that; but if the water come to him and drown him, he drowns not himself. Argal, he that is not guilty of his own death shortens not his own life.
2 CLO.	But is this law?
1 CLO.	Ay, marry, is't; crowner's quest law.
2 CLO.	Will you ha the truth an't? If this had not been a gentlewoman, she should have been buried out a Christian burial.
1 CLO.	Why, there thou say'st; and the more pity that great folk should have count'nance in this world to drown or hang themselves more than their even Christen. Come, my spade. There is no ancient gentlemen but gard'ners, ditchers, and grave-makers; they hold up Adam's profession.
2 CLO.	Was he a gentleman?
1 CLO.	'A was the first that ever bore arms.
2 CLO.	Why, he had none.
1 CLO.	What, art a heathen? How dost thou understand the Scripture? The Scripture says Adam digg'd. Could he dig without arms? I'll put another question to thee. If thou

	answerest me not to the purpose, confess thyself—
2 CLO.	Go to.
1 CLO.	What is he that builds stronger than either the mason, the shipwright, or the carpenter?
2 CLO.	The gallows-maker; for that frame outlives a thousand tenants.
1 CLO.	I like thy wit well; in good faith the gallows does well; but how does it well? It does well to those that do ill. Now thou dost ill to say the gallows is built stronger than the church; argal, the gallows may do well to thee. To 't again, come.
2 CLO.	Who builds stronger than a mason, a shipwright, or a carpenter?
1 CLO.	Ay, tell me that, and unyoke.
2 CLO.	Marry, now I can tell.
1 CLO.	To 't.
2 CLO.	Mass, I cannot tell.

ENTER HAMLET AND HORATIO, AFAR OFF.

1 CLO.	Cudgel thy brains no more about it, for your dull ass will not mend his pace with beating; and when you are ask'd this question next, say 'a grave-maker': the houses he makes lasts till doomsday. Go, get thee to Yaughan; fetch me a stoup of liquor. [*Exit Second Clown.* [*Digs and sings*] In youth, when I did love,

did love,
Methought it was very sweet,
To contract-o-the time for-a my behove,
O, methought there-a-was nothing-a meet.

HAM. Has this fellow no feeling of his business, that
'a sings in grave-making?

HOR. Custom hath made it in him a property of
easiness.

HAM. 'Tis e'en so; the hand of little employment
hath the daintier sense.

1 CLO. [*Sings*] But age, with his stealing steps,
Hath clawed me in his clutch,
And hath shipped me intil the land,
As if I had never been such.

[*Throws up a skull.*

HAM. That skull had a tongue in it, and could sing
once. How the knave jowls it to the ground,
as if 'twere Cain's jawbone, that did the first
murder! This might be the pate of a politician,
which this ass now o'erreaches; one that would
circumvent God, might it not?

HOR. It might, my lord.

HAM. Or of a courtier; which could say 'Good
morrow, sweet lord! How dost thou, sweet
lord?' This might be my Lord Sch-a-one, that
praised my Lord Such-a-one's horse, when 'a
meant to beg it—might it not?

HOR. Ay, my lord.

HAM.   Why, e'en so; and now my Lady Worm's,
         chapless, and knock'd about the mazard with
         a sexton's spade. Here's fine revolution, an
         we had the trick to see't. Did these bones cost
         no more the breeding but to play at loggats
         with them? Mine ache to think on't.

1 CLO.   [*Sings*] A pick-axe and a spade, a spade,
             For and a shrouding sheet:
             O, a pit of clay for to be made
             For such a guest is meet.

                     [*Throws up another skull.*

HAM.   There's another. Why may not that be the
         skull of a lawyer? Where be his quiddities
         now, his quillets, his cases, his tenures, and
         his tricks? Why does he suffer this rude knave
         now to knock him about the sconce with a
         dirty shovel, and will not tell him of his action
         of battery? Hum! This fellow might be in's
         time a great buyer of land, with his statutes,
         his recognizances, his fines, his double
         vouchers, his recoveries. Is this the fine of his
         fines, and the recovery of his recoveries, to
         have his fine pate full of fine dirt? Will his
         vouchers vouch him no more of his purchases,
         and double ones too, than the length and
         breadth of a pair of indentures? The very
         conveyances of his lands will scarcely lie in
         this box; and must th' inheritor himself have
         no more, ha?

HOR.	Not a jot more, my lord.
HAM.	Is not parchment made of sheepskins?
HOR.	Ay, my lord, and of calves' skins too.
HAM.	They are sheep and calves which seek out assurance in that. I will speak to this fellow. Whose grave's this, sirrah?
1 CLO.	Mine, sir.
	[*Sings*] O, a pit of clay for to be made
	For such a guest is meet.
HAM.	I think it be thine indeed, for thou liest in't.
1 CLO.	You lie out on't, sir, and therefore 'tis not yours. For my part, I do not lie in't, yet it is mine.
HAM.	Thou dost lie in't, to be in't and say it is thine; 'tis for the dead, not for the quick; therefore thou liest.
1 CLO.	'Tis a quick lie, sir; 'twill away again from me to you.
HAM.	What man dost thou dig it for?
1 CLO.	For no man, sir.
HAM.	What woman, then?
1 CLO.	For none neither.
HAM.	Who is to be buried in't?
1 CLO.	One that was a woman, sir; but, rest her soul, she's dead.
HAM.	How absolute the knave is! We must speak by the card, or equivocation will undo us. By the Lord, Horatio, this three years I have took

note of it: the age is grown so picked that the
toe of the peasant comes so near the heel of
the courtier, he galls his kibe. How long hast
thou been a grave-maker?

1 CLO. Of all the days i' th' year, I came to't that day
that our last King Hamlet overcame
Fortinbras.

HAM. How long is that since?

1 CLO. Cannot you tell that? Every fool can tell that:
it was that very day that young Hamlet was
born—he that is mad, and sent into England.

HAM. Ay, marry, why was he sent into England?

1 CLO. Why, because 'a was mad: 'a shall recover his
wits there; or, if 'a do not, 'tis no great matter
there.

HAM. Why?

1 CLO. 'Twill not be seen in him there: there the men
are as mad as he.

HAM. How came he mad?

1 CLO. Very strangely, they say.

HAM. How strangely?

1 CLO. Faith, e'en with losing his wits.

HAM. Upon what ground?

1 CLO. Why, here in Denmark. I have been sexton
here, man and boy, thirty years.

HAM. How long will a man lie i' th' earth ere he
rot?

1 CLO. Faith, if 'a be not rotten before 'a die—as we

have many pocky corses now-a-days that will scarce hold the laying in—'a will last you some eight year or nine year. A tanner will last you nine year.

HAM. Why he more than another?

1 CLO. Why, sir, his hide is so tann'd with his trade that 'a will keep out water a great while; and your water is a sore decayer of your whoreson dead body. Here's a skull now; this skull has lien you i' th' earth three and twenty years.

HAM. Whose was it?

1 CLO. A whoreson mad fellow's it was. Whose do you think it was?

HAM. Nay, I know not.

1 CLO. A pestilence on him for a mad rogue! 'A poured a flagon of Rhenish on my head once. This same skull, sir, was, sir, Yorick's skull, the King's jester.

HAM. This?

1 CLO. E'en that.

HAM. Let me see. [*Takes the skull*] Alas, poor Yorick! I knew him, Horatio: a fellow of infinite jest, of most excellent fancy; he hath borne me on his back a thousand times. And now how abhorred in my imagination it is! My gorge rises at it. Here hung those lips that I have kiss'd I know not how oft. Where be your gibes now, your gambols, your songs, your flashes of merriment that were wont to set the table on a roar? Not one now to mock your own grinning—quite chap-fall'n? Now get you to my lady's chamber, and tell her, let her paint an inch thick, to this favour she must come; make her laugh at that. Prithee, Horatio, tell me one thing.

HOR.   What's that, my lord?

HAM.   Dost thou think Alexander look'd a this fashion i' th' earth?

HOR.   E'en so.

HAM.   And smelt so? Pah!

[*Throws down the skull.*

HOR.   E'en so, my lord.

HAM.   To what base uses we may return, Horatio! Why may not imagination trace the noble dust of Alexander till 'a find it stopping a bung-hole?

HOR.   'Twere to consider too curiously to consider so.

HAM.   No, faith, not a jot; but to follow him thither with modesty enough, and likelihood to lead it, as thus: Alexander died, Alexander was buried, Alexander returneth to dust; the dust is earth; of earth we make loam; and why of that loam whereto he was converted might they not stop a beer-barrel?
Imperious Cæsar, dead and turn'd to clay,
Might stop a hole to keep the wind away.

O, that that earth which kept the world in
awe
Should patch a wall t' expel the winter's flaw!
But soft! but soft! awhile. Here comes the
King.

ENTER THE KING, QUEEN, LAERTES, IN FUNERAL
PROCESSION AFTER THE COFFIN, WITH PRIEST AND
LORDS ATTENDANT.

The Queen, the courtiers. Who is this they
follow?
And with such maimed rites? This doth
betoken
The corse they follow did with desperate hand
Fordo it own life. 'Twas of some estate.
Couch we awhile and mark.
                              [*Retiring with Horatio.*

LAER.   What ceremony else?
HAM.   That is Laertes, a very noble youth. Mark.
LAER.   What ceremony else?
PRIEST.   Her obsequies have been as far enlarg'd
           As we have warrantise. Her death was
           doubtful;
           And, but that great command o'ersways the
           order.
           She should in ground unsanctified have lodg'd
           Till the last trumpet; for charitable prayers,
           Shards, flints, and pebbles, should be thrown
           on her;

Yet here she is allow'd her virgin crants,
Her maiden strewments, and the bringing home
Of bell and burial.

LAER.   Must there no more be done?

PRIEST.   No more be done.
           We should profane the service of the dead
           To sing sage requiem and such rest to her
           As to peace-parted souls.

LAER.   Lay her i' th' earth;
           And from her fair and unpolluted flesh
           May violets spring! I tell thee, churlish priest,
           A minist'ring angel shall my sister be
           When thou liest howling.

HAM.   What, the fair Ophelia!

QUEEN.   Sweets to the sweet; farewell!

                                   [*Scattering flowers.*

           I hop'd thou shouldst have been my Hamlet's wife;
           I thought thy bride-bed to have deck'd, sweet maid,
           And not have strew'd thy grave.

LAER.   O, treble woe
           Fall ten times treble on that cursed head
           Whose wicked deed thy most ingenious sense
           Depriv'd thee of! Hold off the earth awhile,
           Till I have caught her once more in mine arms.   [*Leaps into the grave.*

Now pile your dust upon the quick and dead,
Till of this flat a mountain you have made
T' o'er-top old Pelion or the skyish head
Of blue Olympus.

HAM.   [*Advancing*] What is he whose grief
Bears such an emphasis, whose phrase of sorrow
Conjures the wand'ring stars, and makes them stand
Like wonder-wounded hearers? This is I,
Hamlet the Dane.   [*Leaps into the grave.*

LAER.   The devil take thy soul!
                    [*Grappling with him.*

HAM.   Thou pray'st not well.
I prithee take thy fingers from my throat;
For, though I am not splenitive and rash,
Yet have I in me something dangerous,
Which let thy wiseness fear. Hold off thy hand.

KING.   Pluck them asunder.

QUEEN.   Hamlet! Hamlet!

ALL.   Gentlemen!

HOR.   Good my lord, be quiet.
            [*The Attendants part them, and
                they come out of the grave.*

HAM.   Why, I will fight with him upon this theme
Until my eyelids will no longer wag.

QUEEN.   O my son, what theme?

HAM.   I lov'd Ophelia: forty thousand brothers

	Could not, with all their quantity of love, Make up my sum. What wilt thou do for her?
KING.	O, he is mad, Laertes.
QUEEN.	For love of God, forbear him.
HAM.	'Swounds, show me what th'owt do: Woo't weep, woo't fight, woo't fast, woo't tear thyself, Woo't drink up eisel, eat a crocodile? I'll do't. Dost come here to whine? To outface me with leaping in her grave? Be buried quick with her, and so will I; And, if thou prate of mountains, let them throw Millions of acres on us, till our ground, Singeing his pate against the burning zone, Make Ossa like a wart! Nay, an thou'lt mouth, I'll rant as well as thou.
QUEEN.	This is mere madness; And thus awhile the fit will work on him; Anon, as patient as the female dove When that her golden couplets are disclos'd, His silence will sit drooping.
HAM.	Hear you, sir: What is the reason that you use me thus? I lov'd you ever. But it is no matter. Let Hercules himself do what he may,

The cat will mew, and dog will have his day.
[*Exit.*

KING.   I pray thee, good Horatio, wait upon him.
[*Exit Horatio.*
[*To Laertes*] Strengthen your patience in our
last night's speech;
We'll put the matter to the present push.—
Good Gertrude, set some watch over your
son.—
This grave shall have a living monument.
An hour of quiet shortly shall we see;
Till then in patience our proceeding be.
[*Exeunt.*

SCENE II

Elsinore. The Castle.

ENTER HAMLET AND HORATIO.

HAM.   So much for this, sir; now shall you see the
other.
You do remember all the circumstance?
HOR.   Remember it, my lord!
HAM.   Sir, in my heart there was a kind of fighting
That would not let me sleep. Methought I
lay

Worse than the mutines in the bilboes.
Rashly,
And prais'd be rashness for it—let us know,
Our indiscretion sometime serves us well,
When our deep plots do pall; and that should
learn us
There's a divinity that shapes our ends,
Rough-hew them how we will.

HOR.   That is most certain.

HAM.   Up from my cabin,
My sea-gown scarf'd about me, in the dark
Grop'd I to find out them; had my desire;
Finger'd their packet, and in fine withdrew
To mine own room again, making so bold,
My fears forgetting manners, to unseal
Their grand commission; where I found,
Horatio,
Ah, royal knavery! an exact command,
Larded with many several sorts of reasons,
Importing Denmark's health and England's
too,
With, ho! such bugs and goblins in my life—
That, on the supervise, no leisure bated,
No, not to stay the grinding of the axe,
My head should be struck off.

HOR.   Is't possible?

HAM.   Here's the commission; read it at more leisure.
But wilt thou hear now how I did proceed?

HOR.   I beseech you.

HAM.   Being thus benetted round with villainies—
          Ere I could make a prologue to my brains,
          They had begun the play—I sat me down;
          Devis'd a new commission; wrote it fair.
          I once did hold it, as our statists do,
          A baseness to write fair, and labour'd much
          How to forget that learning; but, sir, now
          It did me yeoman's service. Wilt thou know
          Th' effect of what I wrote?

HOR.   Ay, good my lord.

HAM.   An earnest conjuration from the King,
          As England was his faithful tributary,
          As love between them like the palm might
          flourish,
          As peace should still her wheaten garland wear
          And stand a comma 'tween their amities,
          And many such like as-es of great charge,
          That, on the view and knowing of these
          contents,
          Without debatement further more or less,
          He should those bearers put to sudden death,
          Not shriving-time allow'd.

HOR.   How was this seal'd?

HAM.   Why, even in that was heaven ordinant.
          I had my father's signet in my purse,
          Which was the model of that Danish seal;
          Folded the writ up in the form of th' other;
          Subscrib'd it, gave't th' impression, plac'd it
          safely,

The changeling never known. Now, the next day
Was our sea-fight; and what to this was sequent
Thou knowest already.

HOR.   So Guildenstern and Rosencrantz go to't.

HAM.   Why, man, they did make love to this employment;
They are not near my conscience; their defeat
Does by their own insinuation grow;
'Tis dangerous when the baser nature comes
Between the pass and fell incensed points
Of mighty opposites.

HOR.   Why, what a king is this!

HAM.   Does it not, think thee, stand me now upon—
He that hath kill'd my king and whor'd my mother;
Popp'd in between th' election and my hopes;
Thrown out his angle for my proper life,
And with such coz'nage—is't not perfect conscience
To quit him with this arm? And is't not to be damn'd
To let this canker of our nature come
In further evil?

HOR.   It must be shortly known to him from England

What is the issue of the business there.

HAM.   It will be short; the interim is mine,
And a man's life's no more than to say 'one'.
But I am very sorry, good Horatio,
That to Laertes I forgot myself;
For by the image of my cause I see
The portraiture of his. I'll court his favours.
But sure the bravery of his grief did put me
Into a tow'ring passion.

HOR.   Peace; who comes here?

ENTER YOUNG OSRIC.

OSR.   Your lordship is right welcome back to
Denmark.

HAM.   I humbly thank you, sir. [*Aside to Horatio*]
Dost know this water-fly?

HOR.   [*Aside to Hamlet*] No, my good lord.

HAM.   [*Aside to Horatio*] Thy state is the more
gracious; for 'tis a vice to know him. He hath
much land, and fertile. Let a beast be lord of
beasts, and his crib shall stand at the king's
mess. 'Tis a chough; but, as I say, spacious in
the possession of dirt.

OSR.   Sweet lord, if your lordship were at leisure, I
should impart a thing to you from his
Majesty.

HAM.   I will receive it, sir, with all diligence of spirit.
Put your bonnet to his right use; 'tis for the

	head.
OSR.	I thank your lordship; it is very hot.
HAM.	No, believe me, 'tis very cold; the wind is northerly.
OSR.	It is indifferent cold, my lord, indeed.
HAM.	But yet methinks it is very sultry and hot for my complexion.
OSR.	Exceedingly, my lord; it is very sultry, as 'twere—I cannot tell how. But, my lord, his Majesty bade me signify to you that 'a has laid a great wager on your head. Sir, this is the matter—
HAM.	I beseech you, remember.
	[*Hamlet moves him to put on his hat.*
OSR.	Nay, good my lord; for my ease, in good faith. Sir, here is newly come to court Laertes; believe me, an absolute gentleman, full of most excellent differences, of very soft society and great showing. Indeed, to speak feelingly of him, he is the card or calendar of gentry, for you shall find in him the continent of what part a gentleman would see.
HAM.	Sir, his definement suffers no perdition in you; though, I know, to divide him inventorially would dozy th' arithmetic of memory, and yet but yaw neither in respect of his quick sail. But, in the verity of extolment, I take him to be a soul of great article, and his

	infusion of such dearth and rareness as, to make true diction of him, his semblable is his mirror, and who else would trace him, his umbrage, nothing more.
OSR.	Your lordship speaks most infallibly of him.
HAM.	The concernancy, sir? Why do we wrap the gentleman in our more rawer breath?
OSR.	Sir?
HOR.	[*Aside to Hamlet*] Is't not possible to understand in another tongue? You will to't, sir, really.
HAM.	What imports the nomination of this gentleman?
OSR.	Of Laertes?
HOR.	[*Aside*] His purse is empty already; all's golden words are spent.
HAM.	Of him, sir.
OSR.	I know you are not ignorant—
HAM.	I would you did, sir; yet, in faith, if you did, it would not much approve me. Well, sir.
OSR.	You are not ignorant of what excellence Laertes is—
HAM.	I dare not confess that, lest I should compare with him in excellence; but to know a man well were to know himself.
OSR.	I mean, sir, for his weapon; but in the imputation laid on him by them, in his meed he's unfellowed.

HAM.   What's his weapon?

OSR.   Rapier and dagger.

HAM.   That's two of his weapons—but well.

OSR.   The King, sir, hath wager'd with him six Barbary horses; against the which he had impon'd, as I take it, six French rapiers and poniards, with their assigns, as girdle, hangers, and so—three of the carriages, in faith, are very dear to fancy, very responsive to the hilts, most delicate carriages, and of very liberal conceit.

HAM.   What call you the carriages?

HOR.   [*Aside to Hamlet*] I knew you must be edified by the margent ere you had done.

OSR.   The carriages, sir, are the hangers.

HAM.   The phrase would be more germane to the matter if we could carry a cannon by our sides. I would it might be hangers till then. But on: six Barbary horses against six French swords, their assigns, and three liberal conceited carriages; that's the French bet against the Danish. Why is this all impon'd, as you call it?

ORS.   The King, sir, hath laid, sir, that in a dozen passes between yourself and him he shall not exceed you three hits; he hath laid on twelve for nine, and it would come to immediate trial if your lordship would vouchsafe the answer.

HAM.   How if I answer no?

OSR.   I mean, my lord, the opposition of your person in trial.

HAM.   Sir, I will walk here in the hall. If it please his Majesty, it is the breathing time of day with me; let the foils be brought, the gentleman willing, and the King hold his purpose, I will win for him an I can; if not, I will gain nothing but my shame and the odd hits.

OSR.   Shall I redeliver you e'en so?

HAM.   To this effect, sir, after what flourish your nature will.

OSR.   I commend my duty to your lordship.

HAM.   Yours, yours. [*Exit Osric*] He does well to commend it himself; there are no tongues else for's turn.

HOR.   This lapwing runs away with the shell on his head.

HAM.   'A did comply, sir, with his dug before 'a suck'd it. Thus has he, and many more of the same bevy, that I know the drossy age dotes on, only got the tune of the time and outward habit of encounter—a kind of yesty collection, which carries them through and through the most fann'd and winnowed opinions; and do but blow them to their trial, the bubbles are out.

ENTER A LORD.

LORD.   My lord, his Majesty commended him to
          you by young Osric, who brings back to him
          that you attend him in the hall. He sends to
          know if your pleasure hold to play with
          Laertes, or that you will take longer time.

HAM.   I am constant to my purposes; they follow
          the king's pleasure: if his fitness speaks, mine
          is ready now—or whensoever, provided I be
          so able as now.

LORD.   The King and Queen and all are coming
          down.

HAM.   In happy time.

LORD.   The Queen desires you to use some gentle
          entertainment to Laertes before you fall to
          play.

HAM.   She well instructs me.   [*Exit Lord.*

HOR.   You will lose this wager, my lord.

HAM.   I do not think so; since he went into France I
          have been in continual practice. I shall win at
          the odds. But thou wouldst not think how
          ill all's here about my heart; but it is no matter.

HOR.   Nay, good my lord—

HAM.   It is but foolery; but it is such a kind of gain-
          giving as would perhaps trouble a woman.

HOR.   If your mind dislike anything, obey it. I will
          forestall their repair hither, and say you are
          not fit.

HAM.   Not a whit, we defy augury: there is a special
          providence in the fall of a sparrow. If it be
          now, 'tis not to come; if it be not to come, it
          will be now; if it be not now, yet it will
          come—the readiness is all. Since no man owes
          of aught he leaves, what is't to leave betimes?
          Let be.

*A TABLE PREPARED. TRUMPETS, DRUMS, AND OFFICERS
WITH CUSHIONS, FOILS AND DAGGERS. ENTER KING,
      QUEEN, LAERTES, AND ALL THE STATE.*

KING.   Come, Hamlet, come, and take this hand from
          me. [*The King puts Laertes's hand into Hamlet's.*
HAM.   Give me your pardon, sir. I have done you
          wrong;
          But pardon 't, as you are a gentleman.
          This presence knows,
          And you must needs have heard how I am
          punish'd
          With a sore distraction. What I have done
          That might your nature, honour, and
          exception,
          Roughly awake, I here proclaim was madness.
          Was 't Hamlet wrong'd Laertes? Never
          Hamlet.
          If Hamlet from himself be ta'en away,
          And when he's not himself does wrong
          Laertes,
          Then Hamlet does it not, Hamlet denies it.

Who does it, then? His madness. If't be so,
Hamlet is of the faction that is wrong'd;
His madness is poor Hamlet's enemy.
Sir, in this audience,
Let my disclaiming from a purpos'd evil
Free me so far in your most generous
thoughts
That I have shot my arrow o'er the house
And hurt my brother.

LAER.   I am satisfied in nature,
Whose motive in this case should stir me
most
To my revenge; but in my terms of honour
I stand aloof, and will no reconcilement
Till by some elder masters of known honour
I have a voice and precedent of peace
To keep my name ungor'd—but till that
time
I do receive your offer'd love like love,
And will not wrong it.

HAM.   I embrace it freely;
And will this brother's wager frankly play.
Give us the foils. Come on.

LAER.   Come, one for me.

HAM.   I'll be your foil, Laertes; in mine ignorance
Your skill shall, like a star i' th' darkest night,
Stick fiery off indeed.

LAER.   You mock me, sir.

HAM.   No, by this hand.

KING.   Give them the foils, young Osric.
Cousin Hamlet,
You know the wager?

HAM.   Very well, my lord;
Your Grace has laid the odds a' th' weaker side.

KING.   I do not fear it: I have seen you both;
But since he's better'd, we have therefore odds.

LAER.   This is too heavy; let me see another.

HAM.   This likes me well. These foils have all a length?   [*They prepare to play.*

OSR.   Ay, my good lord.

KING.   Set me the stoups of wine upon that table.
If Hamlet give the first or second hit
Or quit in answer of the third exchange,
Let all the battlements their ordnance fire;
The King shall drink to Hamlet's letter breath,
And in the cup an union shall he throw,
Richer than that which four successive kings
In Denmark's crown have worn. Give me the cups;
And let the kettle to the trumpet speak,
The trumpet to the cannoneer without,
The cannons to the heavens, the heaven to earth,
'Now the King drinks to Hamlet'. Come, begin—

	And you, the judges, bear a wary eye.
HAM.	Come on, sir.
LAER.	Come, my lord. *[They play.*
HAM.	One.
LAER.	No.
HAM.	Judgment?
OSR.	A hit, a very palpable hit.
LAER.	Well, again.
KING.	Stay, give me drink. Hamlet, this pearl is thine;
	Here's to thy health.

                    [Drum, trumpets, and shot.

	Give him the cup.
HAM.	I'll play this bout first; set it by awhile.
	Come. *[They play.*
	Another hit; what say you?
LAER.	A touch, a touch, I do confess't.
KING.	Our son shall win.
QUEEN.	He's fat, and scant of breath.
	Here, Hamlet, take my napkin, rub thy brows.
	The Queen carouses to thy fortune, Hamlet.
HAM.	Good madam!
KING.	Gertrude, do not drink.
QUEEN.	I will, my lord; I pray you pardon me.
KING.	*[Aside]* It is the poison'd cup; it is too late.
HAM.	I dare not drink yet, madam; by and by.
QUEEN.	Come, let me wipe thy face.
LAER.	My lord, I'll hit him now.

KING.   I do not think't.

LAER.   [*Aside*] And yet it is almost against my
conscience.

HAM.   Come, for the third. Laertes, you do but dally;
I pray you pass with your best violence;
I am afeard you make a wanton of me.

LAER.   Say you so? Come on.   [*They play.*

OSR.   Nothing, neither way.

LAER.   Have at you now! [*Laertes wounds
Hamlet: then, in scuffling, they change
rapiers, and Hamlet wounds Laertes.*

KING.   Part them; they are incens'd.

HAM.   Nay, come again.   [*The Queen falls.*

OSR.   Look to the Queen there, ho!

HOR.   They bleed on both sides. How is it, my lord?

OSR.   How is't, Laertes?

LAER.   Why, as a woodcock, to mine own springe,
Osric;
I am justly kill'd with mine own treachery.

HAM.   How does the Queen?

KING.   She swoons to see them bleed.

QUEEN.   No, no, the drink, the drink! O my dear
Hamlet!
The drink, the drink! I am poison'd.   [*Dies.*

HAM.   O, villainy! Ho! let the door be lock'd.
Treachery! seek it out.   [*Laertes falls.*

LAER.   It is here, Hamlet. Hamlet, thou art slain;
No med'cine in the world can do thee good;

In thee there is not half an hour's life;
The treacherous instrument is in thy hand,
Unbated and envenom'd. The foul practice
Hath turn'd itself on me; lo, here I lie,
Never to rise again. Thy mother's poison'd.
I can no more. The King, the King's to blame.

HAM. The point envenom'd too!
Then, venom, to thy work.   [*Stabs the King.*

ALL. Treason! treason!

KING. O, yet defend me, friends; I am but hurt.

HAM. Here, thou incestuous, murd'rous, damned
Dane,
Drink off this potion. Is thy union here?
Follow my mother.   [*King dies.*

LAER. He is justly serv'd:
It is a poison temper'd by himself.
Exchange forgiveness with me, noble Hamlet.
Mine and my father's death come not upon
thee,
Nor thine on me!   [*Dies.*

HAM. Heaven make thee free of it! I follow thee.
I am dead, Horatio. Wretched queen, adieu!
You that look pale and tremble at this chance,
That are but mutes or audience to this act,
Had I but time, as this fell sergeant Death
Is strict in his arrest, O, I could tell you—
But let it be. Horatio, I am dead:
Thou livest; report me and my cause aright
To the unsatisfied.

HOR.   Never believe it.
        I am more an antique Roman than a Dane;
        Here's yet some liquor left.

HAM.   As th'art a man,
        Give me the cup. Let go. By heaven, I'll ha't.
        O God! Horatio, what a wounded name,
        Things standing thus unknown, shall live behind me!
        If thou didst ever hold me in thy heart,
        Absent thee from felicity awhile,
        And in this harsh world draw thy breath in pain,
        To tell my story.
                [*March afar off, and shot within.*
                What warlike noise is this?

OSR.   Young Fortinbras, with conquest come from Poland,
        To th' ambassadors of England gives
        This warlike volley.

HAM.   O, I die, Horatio!
        The potent poison quite o'er-crows my spirit.
        I cannot live to hear the news from England,
        But I do prophesy th' election lights
        On Fortinbras; he has my dying voice.
        So tell him, with th' occurrents, more and less,
        Which have solicited—the rest is silence.
                        [*Dies.*

HOR.   Now cracks a noble heart. Good night, sweet
            prince,
            And flights of angels sing thee to thy rest!
                          [March within.
            Why does the drum come hither?

ENTER FORTINBRAS AND ENGLISH AMBASSADORS,
WITH DRUM, COLOURS, AND ATTENDANTS.

FORT.   Where is this sight?
HOR.   What is it you would see?
            If aught of woe or wonder, cease your search.
FORT.   This quarry cries on havoc. O proud death,
            What feast is toward in thine eternal cell
            That thou so many princes at a shot
            So bloodily hast struck?
1 AMB.   The sight is dismal;
            And our affairs from England come too late:
            The ears are senseless that should give us
            hearing
            To tell him his commandment is fulfill'd,
            That Rosencrantz and Guildenstern are dead.
            Where should we have our thanks?
HOR.   Not from his mouth,
            Had it th' ability of life to thank you:
            He never gave commandment for their death.
            But since, so jump upon this bloody question,
            You from the Polack wars, and you from
            England,

Are here arrived, give order that these bodies
High on a stage be placed to the view;
And let me speak to th' yet unknowing world
How these things came about. So shall you
hear
Of carnal, bloody, and unnatural acts;
Of accidental judgments, casual slaughters;
Of deaths put on by cunning and forc'd cause;
And, in this upshot, purposes mistook
Fall'n on th' inventors' heads—and this can I
Truly deliver.

FORT.   Let us haste to hear it,
And call the noblest to the audience.
For me, with sorrow I embrace my fortune;
I have some rights of memory in this
kingdom,
Which now to claim my vantage doth invite
me.

HOR.   Of that I shall have also cause to speak,
And from his mouth whose voice will draw
on more.
But let this same be presently perform'd,
Even while men's minds are wild, lest more
mischance
On plots and errors happen.

FORT.   Let four captains
Bear Hamlet like a soldier to the stage;
For he was likely, had he been put on,

To have prov'd most royal; and for his passage
The soldier's music and the rite of war
Speak loudly for him.
Take up the bodies. Such a sight as this
Becomes the field, but here shows much
amiss.
Go, bid the soldiers shoot.

                              [*Exeunt marching.*
                         A peal of ordnance shot off.

www.ingramcontent.com/pod-product-compliance
Lightning Source LLC
Chambersburg PA
CBHW031956010726
47493CB00007B/2223